Just Following Orders:

Escape from Guerrilla Warfare in 1863

Dee Ann Miller

with assistant Nancy Ketter

FREE chapter-by-chapter lesson plans,
study helps, and fun activities, check out:
http://justfollowingorders.takecourage.org

This book is dedicated to my five wonderful grandchildren

—Micah, Malachi, Haley, Matthew, and Kellyn.

*May you each continually live for peace
in every aspect of life.*

Cover by Eddie Egesi
Phone: 240-839-0882
mregesi@yahoo.com

Illustrated by Nancy Ketter,
Lydia Lane, and Madison Kuhle

List of Characters

(The italicized names are actual historical figures in the story.)

The Carter family: As the story opens, Joshua is about to turn 14. He's the oldest of five children. Parents are Cyrus and Lucy Carter, siblings are Billy (age 9), Tom (6), Jenny (3), and Baby George (not yet a year old). Homer Carter is Joshua's grandfather.

The Mullins family: They are the Carters' neighbors. Sam and Olivia are the parents of Betsy (8) and Mary (6).

Andrew Owsley—Joshua's good friend and fishing buddy
Uncle John—Andrew's uncle
William Dyer—Andrew's cousin, a Union soldier
George Manning—a Confederate soldier
Rev. George Miller—the Carter family's minister
Sadie Miller—the minister's wife

The Wornall family: *John* and *Eliza* are the parents of *Frank* (8) and two very young daughters. *Ednie* is a toddler; *Sallie*'s less than a year old. Three of their four servants were all formerly household slaves:

Aunt Molly—Wornall's cook and housekeeper
Jim—Aunt Molly's young adult son
Pete—Jim's younger brother (9)
Hans—a "white" hired hand of German descent
Rev. Thomas Johnson and his wife *Sarah*—parents of Eliza Wornall. Rev. Johnson operated the Shawnee Indian Mission and Training School for many years with his wife's assistance.

Solomon and Alice—two teenage friends who are guests of the Johnson's
Mark—a cabin attendant on the steamboat *Prosperity*
Hector Collins—son of the owners of a boarding house in Hannibal, Missouri
Esther—singer on the steamboat *Sweet Betsy from Pike*
Aunt Gladys—a relative of Olivia Mullins
Mr. Howe—abolitionist, editor, teacher, and founder of Howe's Academy in Mt. Pleasant, Iowa
Mrs. Johnson—a freedwoman and employee of Lucy Carter
Hosea and Truman Johnson—sons of Mrs. Johnson and friends of the Carter brothers

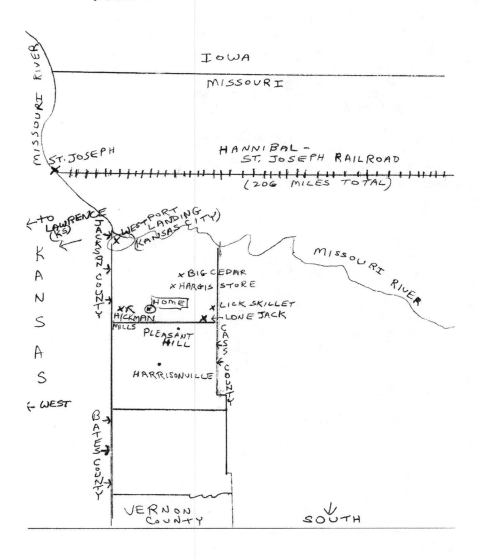

NORTH ↑

IOWA

MISSOURI

MISSOURI RIVER

ST. JOSEPH

HANNIBAL -
ST. JOSEPH RAILROAD
(206 MILES TOTAL)

←to LAWRENCE (KS)

WESTPORT LANDING (KANSAS CITY)

MISSOURI RIVER

KANSAS

JACKSON COUNTY

×BIG CEDAR
×HARGIS STORE

HOME

×× HICKMAN MILLS

× LICK SKILLET
× LONE JACK

PLEASANT HILL

CASS COUNTY

• HARRISONVILLE

← WEST

BATES COUNTY

VERNON COUNTY

SOUTH ↓

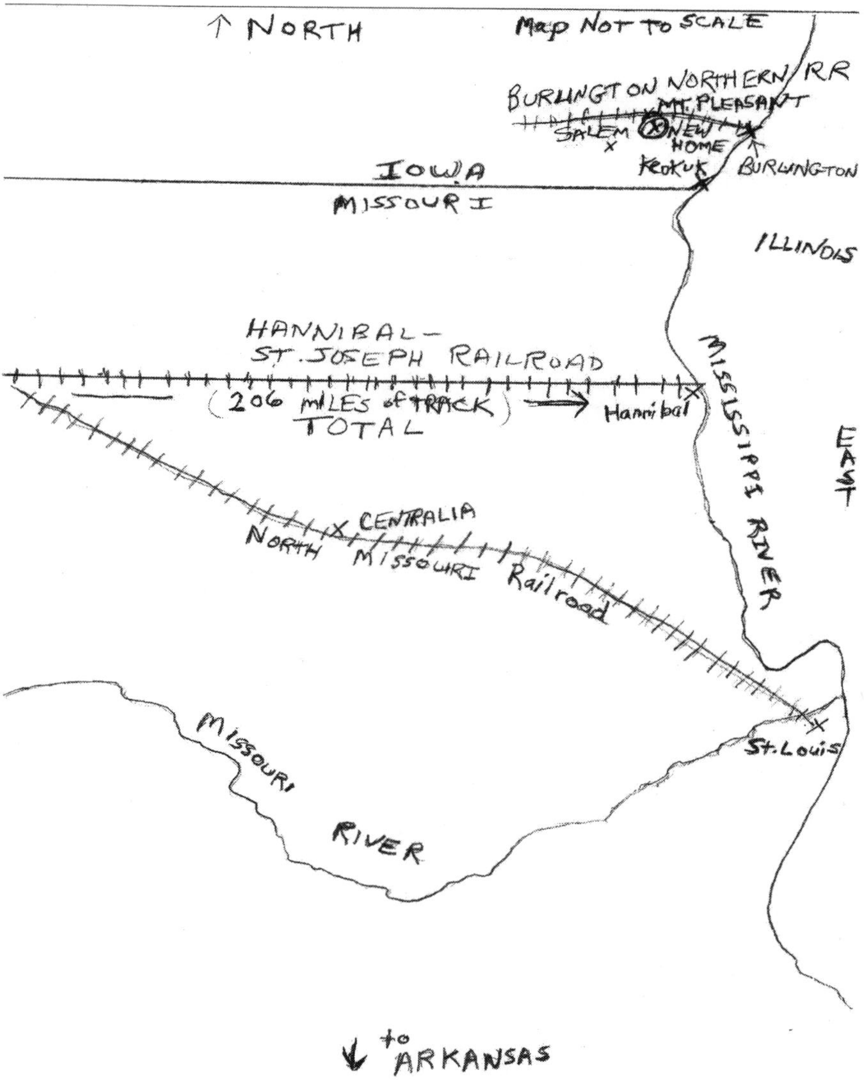

↑ NORTH
Map Not To SCALE
BURLINGTON NORTHERN RR
MT. PLEASANT
SALEM
NEW HOME
KEOKUK
BURLINGTON
IOWA
MISSOURI
ILLINOIS
HANNIBAL-
ST. JOSEPH RAILROAD
(206 miles of TRACK TOTAL)
Hannibal
MISSISSIPPI RIVER
EAST
CENTRALIA
NORTH MISSOURI Railroad
St. Louis
MISSOURI RIVER
to ARKANSAS

1

In late summer of 1863, few people of western Missouri blamed William Quantrill for the mess they were in. Many saw him as a hero. Some still do. It didn't matter that he'd recently torn through the city of Lawrence, Kansas, with 400 crazed and drunken men, leaving 250 children fatherless. Those people had it coming, folks on the other side of the border said. In their eyes, the Union's heavy-handed tactics following the raid were the sole reason that 20,000 destitute Missourians in over three counties were about to be homeless on hot, dusty roads.

Grandpa Carter didn't see it that way. Neither did his oldest grandson, Joshua, who would be turning fourteen in only two weeks. Cyrus Carter, Joshua's father, wouldn't agree either—if he was still around to talk, that is.

To the Carters, there were more than two sides to this story. They hated slavery as much as anyone, but had a low tolerance for nonsense. And there was plenty of nonsense to go around. It came from both armies, as well as law-breaking Confederate bush-whackers, violent abolitionists, and thieves on each side of the border, who were running off with anything not tied down and half that was. Such nonsense was what kept people too riled up to talk safely about the big issues.

Young people everywhere were supposed to think of war as the greatest adventure of their lives. Of course, it helped if their parents agreed. Adults and children alike must always show loyalty to those in charge. That's what it meant to be patriotic. In the South, officers of the Confederacy were in charge. In Missouri, where people were divided, the Union was *officially* in charge. Yet some Missourians were very hard folks for the Union to control.

From his school lessons around the kitchen table, Joshua

1

often heard about violence and oppression. Those were the real problems, Ma said. Slavery was the most obvious example of oppression, and often violence went with it. Another was the way Indians were being treated—Grandpa Carter made sure they got that part. It didn't make sense to him that the Union was fighting a war to stop slavery at the same time it was violently pushing Indians off their land.

Pa tried to teach the same way. He'd still be trying if he hadn't had to close the little schoolhouse two years ago. Of course, he could never say a lot he wanted to say at school or anywhere else. Somebody would be fighting mad, no matter what he said!

"That's just the way it is with guerrilla warfare," Pa explained to his sons. "We're not just in a war here, boys. Never know who we can trust, even among our neighbors, or who may come after us if we say or do the wrong thing."

These explanations and warnings did nothing to ease Joshua's mind or answer the question foremost in his mind. When was the terror ever going to end? That's what everyone was asking.

It really didn't matter how the Carters felt the Sunday afternoon of September 6, 1863. First thing tomorrow morning they'd be out on the road, among the homeless, same as all their neighbors. What's more, barring some miracle, Cyrus wouldn't be with them.

For the day after the Lawrence massacre, he'd come out of hiding and made a beeline to Kansas despite being on the wanted lists of both the Union army and the bushwhackers, of which Quantrill was "king." What else could he do with his sister, Joshua's Aunt Charlotte, likely among the widows in Lawrence, left alone with a whole brood of little boys to rear?

As it turned out, Aunt Charlotte was one of the lucky ones. Not her brother, though. Cyrus Carter's family had seen neither hide nor hair of him for over two weeks.

2

"Joshua, you'll be lucky to keep that stubborn, old mule on the road." Lucy Carter's blue eyes glowed as she elbowed her oldest son and looked lovingly at nine-month-old George. "Just be sure my babies don't end up in a ditch beside the cart—that's all I ask."

"Aw, Ma! Keeping Old Nelly on the straight and narrow is a tall order," Joshua said in a fake, falsetto voice that had the rest of the family rolling with laughter. Just six months earlier, such high-pitched sounds came frequently, without warning. Back then, they were no laughing matter. How he'd hated sounding like a silly, ten-year-old girl! But for weeks now, the steady, bass tones resonating from deep in his throat, served as a constant reassurance, reminding him of his father.

The voice wasn't all he was faking. He didn't know if he was more terrified and saddened than his mother and grandfather, but he was doing his best to join them in keeping the younger kids from sensing the depth of his feelings.

Jenny, Tom, and Billy were all perched across the kitchen table as Lucy took a break from packing to let lunch settle. At that moment, a stranger coming by might have wondered who was having more fun, the adults or the children.

"What's the funny name of the town near the border where we'll be stopping?" nine-year-old Billy asked, as if their forced eviction was equal to being offered an ocean voyage. He had no idea how hard it would be getting past the guerrillas, not to speak of the roaring Missouri River further north. Well, what could you expect from a boy who'd never been more than six miles from home?

"The place is Lick Skillet," shouted Joshua. Billy had asked the same question four times since yesterday at noon. Couldn't he remember anything? Why didn't he study the map like his big brother, who'd carefully memorized every stream since Mr. Mullins dropped off the hand-drawn masterpiece last Friday?

"'Ick Skillet?'" Six-year-old Tom giggled as he tried out the silly name. With two front teeth missing, that kid had a hard time starting words with an L.

"So will there be a skillet to lick?" Jenny chimed in, her diction clear as the blue eyes, shining like diamonds, same as Lucy's.

"I'm sure there will be, knowing your mother," Grandpa assured his only granddaughter. He swung her up on one arm and reached for Baby George with the other. "Let's go out and play in the barn, Tom," he called over his shoulder. "I think your ma can put the older boys to work a lot easier if we get out of her hair."

As soon as Joshua finished washing dishes, he took off to the barn, too. He had a pail of water, a bar of homemade lye soap, and clear instructions on scrubbing the mule cart. It wouldn't stay clean long. Still, Ma insisted on having the outside bright and shiny to start their three-week trek.

More importantly, she wanted him to concentrate on the inside. No need to explain why. He himself had used the nasty thing just last week to haul manure out to the onion patch. Ma would never hear of having fresh-washed quilts, food, and dishes in such filth.

Scrubbing he could do automatically, same as daydreaming. Lately he'd done a lot of dreaming at all hours—mostly going back to when life was simpler. Like in 1861, before parents quit sending their kids to school on account of not having the fees or just wanting to keep a closer eye on their children. Their worries weren't only about the dangers on the road. Many boys, more zealous than their parents wished them to be, were running off even before twelve, to join one army or the other.

Joshua wondered if there were other boys in Jackson County

4

who felt like he did about a lot of things. It was impossible to know. He'd not seen any of his old friends long enough for a conversation in over a year. Some were off fighting, chances are with Quantrill. Others were dead. He shuddered at the thought.

Finishing one side of the cart, he thought of Aunt Charlotte. She and Uncle Spencer had arrived as some of the first settlers in Lawrence, back in 1854. They were determined to help stop the spread of slavery by making Kansas a free state.

Of course, many Missourians weren't happy about that idea at all. Rural Missouri depended on their slaves. They needed human "property" to be valued just like corn or hemp. Otherwise, how could they get good prices when they chose to sell? Besides, no farmer could produce much hemp without free labor. Losing their slaves was unthinkable!

The citizens in town depended on their slaves, too. They needed help to keep house and prepare the fine meals they put on the table as much as rural folks. Plus, without slavery, the cost of keeping businesses going would soar. How would they ever manage to train their horses, sew their clothes, build their wagons, houses, and furniture? This system, they'd inherited. They knew no other way to live. Without it, as they saw things, they'd be as destitute, or worse, than the slaves their businesses helped to support!

Lots of people who didn't own slaves—people in Missouri and far away, up north—agreed that prices might rise without slavery. Abolitionists said it didn't matter; slavery had to go, anyway. Their cries got louder and louder as the voices of pro-slavery rose, trying to match the outcries of the opposition.

Then, starting with Lincoln's election in November, 1860, there was some big happening every month for four months in succession. Each new happening created more tension. In December, South Carolina became the first state to leave the Union. In January, much to the disappointment of pro-slavery advocates across the nation, Kansas entered the Union as a free state. Then, in February, the Confederate States of America was formed. The Great Rebellion was on. As far as Missouri was concerned, it was all Kansas' fault with the "capitol city" of the trouble being Lawrence.

Many abolitionists like Uncle Spencer were already helping the slaves find their way to freedom without violence. The thriving underground railroad provided temporary safe places for slaves who had managed to sneak away from their masters, some who were coming into Kansas, eager to join the Union Army.

Yet some abolitionists didn't hesitate to kill slave masters in the process. There were no laws against slavery in Missouri. So this made these jayhawkers thieves and murderers, same as bushwhackers. To "protect their property," many slaves were taken further south where they were often sold into an even harder life.

There was a third group of Kansans, considered by Missourians to be worst of all. These were known as Jennison's Jayhawkers. Charles Jennison was "king" of this group. They cared nothing about slavery, but simply raided smaller communities for the sole purpose of carrying off loot to make a personal profit. In fact, Quantrill claimed the antics of Jennison's men to be among the reasons for the August 21 raid on Lawrence, where he was certain much of the loot could be found.

Quantrill said he was tired of arrogant abolitionists. Truth is Confederates thought all Kansans were arrogant, no matter which of the three groups they were in.

"An eye for an eye and a tooth for a tooth," they said, quoting a favorite verse from the Old Testament, used for centuries to justify revenge. To them, it was a good code to live by since many had witnessed the murder of their own family members.

Yet the raid only made things much worse. Right away "the men of Kansas" shot across the border in retaliation, cranking up the heat—literally. They torched houses, and shot Missouri men and boys in their own front yards. News spread like a prairie fire.

Something had to be done, as the Union saw it. That something was Order Number 11, issued on August 25 by General Ewing, commander of the District of the Border in Kansas City. He was evacuating the entire population of more than three counties. With nobody around to feed them, he reasoned that the bushwhackers would soon head south like a bunch of roaches.

Grandpa Carter was skeptical. Those guys weren't going to be chased off so easily. Meanwhile folks out on the roads would be in danger more than if the Union left well enough alone.

"Order Number 11?" Joshua kept saying. "Heck, there's nothing orderly about it."

Most disturbing, President Lincoln had approved the orders. That was especially hard for a boy whose father and grandfather were among the few in Jackson County who voted for Lincoln in the 1860 election.

Grandpa said it reminded him of an entire school getting detention when the teacher couldn't decide who the troublemakers were. Yet this was much more serious than detention. Maybe it would make things safer someday. But in the next few weeks, between the sweltering heat, hunger, and danger on the roads, the suffering would be unimaginable. It would be especially hard on small children and the elderly. There was nothing fair about it.

The deadline for completing the evacuation was midnight on Wednesday, September 9. That's why they must be organized and ready to roll right after breakfast tomorrow. Otherwise, they'd never get to the county line in time, and they weren't chancing that. Violation of Order No. 11 carried serious consequences.

Jenny and Tom squealed with delight as they tumbled in the hay a few feet from the cart. Grandpa, looking exhausted. He just sat in a corner of the barn, watching the children while Baby George tried to pick up a squirming kitten.

As Joshua went to the well for a bucket of fresh water, the little ones' joy made him wish fleetingly that Ma wouldn't be so dogmatic. It would be much easier to go to a military station to wait it out. Even if the wait turned out to be for months or years. Some people were daring to ask permission to do that, and some were getting it. Ma wouldn't even try.

The Carter's chances were slim, anyway—even if Pa had signed up for the draft, like the Enrollment Act required. The bushwhackers had gotten breakfast and a whole wagon load of loot just days ago. Ma had let them in the door without protest to keep them from causing more trouble. That alone could give reason for Union officers to label the Carters "disloyal."

Anyway, Lucy Carter wouldn't think of having *her* family living as refugees, risking disease, starvation, robbery, or assault in such crowded conditions. She already made that clear. No need to argue with her. They would take their chances going to eastern Iowa, with the help of the Mullins family, their closest neighbors and long-time friends.

It made Joshua tired, just thinking about it. The trip would require a minimum of three weeks' travel with all but the smallest children having to walk part way. They couldn't expect to cover more than ten miles in one day, even if Old Nelly and their two milk cows fully cooperated.

Yet, Iowa sounded good in many ways. He supposed it would be worth all the trouble if they made it. Best of all, there wouldn't be terrorists there. They could play outdoors and start back to school again. Just getting a good night's sleep would be a welcome change for him.

Before the first snow, Mr. Mullins said they'd all be settled in the town of Salem, where he and his wife Olivia had once lived. The warm letters they got from relatives and friends there made them certain the Carters would also be welcome.

All afternoon, whenever he stopped to think of Pa, Joshua's heart pounded. Many a night for the past year, he'd listened from the loft, catching things his parents didn't want him to hear. Worst of all were stories about decaying bodies hanging from trees, being found almost every day with no hope of identifying them.

Those conversations occurred whenever Pa sensed it safe enough to sneak home from his hiding place after dark for a few hours. He always left before daybreak with his arms full of supplies and his head filled with any news Lucy might have.

Others might be avoiding the draft because they were scared or lazy. Cyrus Carter had other reasons. The loss of precious lives on both sides, involving all races, was just too high a price to pay, he insisted. Though he longed to see slavery end immediately, he believed Americans should have been able to find a peaceful solution. In fact, he believed they still could if men would only lay down their guns and start talking respectfully to one another.

"I'll always be willing to die for what I believe," he told his sons. "I'm just not willing to kill for it." This made Cyrus Carter a very rare Missourian, though a courageous one in his son's eyes. Yet it didn't make things one bit easy for the family, only made their life more dangerous.

Late in the afternoon, while hoisting a keg of cornmeal into the front of the cart, Joshua thought how nice it would be to still have two horses and a wagon like the Mullins still did. They were among the fortunate, though. Due to high demand, horses were the most likely thing to be stolen these days.

Of course, he knew Pa had needed the wagon in Lawrence, probably for hauling building supplies, as an ambulance or hearse, and a place to sleep. The Carters would have to get by, he told himself, leaning on one another, making do with what they had left, as they had all his life.

Horses hooves! Anxiously, he ran to the barn door. Scooping up his baby brother, now crawling at his feet, he darted toward the house before glancing back. "Grandpa!" he shouted. "Mr. Mullins is on the front porch. From the look on his face, I'd say something is terribly wrong."

3

Now, as the 6th day of September ended and the 7th began, Joshua was trying to absorb the shattering news as he lay on the bare floor of the loft in the cozy, little house he called home. According to Mr. Mullins, seventeen-year-old Andrew Owsley had been shot in cold blood yesterday while taking a wagon to his grandparents for them to pack.

Five older men had been captured with him and all shot at the same time. They were only three miles inside Jackson County. A grave was dug quickly—just one grave for all six. They were laid side by side. No caskets and no time for a funeral since relatives feared jayhawkers, claiming to be agents of the Union, might soon be back to kill others.

The tragedy would forever be known in Jackson County as "The Lone Jack Massacre." To Joshua, now lying awake next to his sleeping grandpa on the bare wooden floor, it was the saddest day he'd ever known, the day his best fishing buddy had lost his life while just following orders.

Plans for going through Lick Skillet were cancelled. Just too dangerous, Mr. Mullins declared. After delivering the news, he left to go home and prepare a new map.

"Might as well get used to plans changing," Grandpa told the children. "At times like this, the only thing that holds a family together is love. Don't count on anything else for a while."

Grandpa usually didn't talk that way. Love was something he showed in his voice, his gentle touch, and helpfulness; but it seemed that his love was too sacred to speak. Yet just being around him could make a kid feel calm and confident. Even at night, with danger all around and the sweltering heat in the loft he and Joshua shared, that old man slept like a baby.

Well, comfort wasn't particularly high on Joshua's list of priorities that night. It hadn't been all year, unless you counted the comfort of a full stomach. And sleeping was way down his list, though according to Ma, it should be near the top. He fell asleep often, comfort or no comfort, frequently and unintentionally, in the strangest positions, at the oddest hours, usually in broad daylight. For only in daylight could he depend on others to be awake, constantly watching for trouble.

Neither his parents nor his grandfather knew of his strategy or his fears. Boys were to be brave, not talk about their feelings like sissy girls were always doing. So the last thing he'd ever reveal was that he often cried far into the night, though never as much as he had for the last hour.

Ma would be most upset if she knew how he fought sleep, always hearing two voices—one telling him to be wide awake, the other tempting him to dose off. Tonight, the warning voice was far louder than its rival.

There were so many things he would miss in their cozy abode, starting with this tiny spot overlooking the kitchen. Below him, in the hallway, was a small bookcase holding countless, irreplaceable treasures. It was Pa's, built years ago by Grandpa, and now stacked nearly to the ceiling with books brought home when the school closed. Sadly, Joshua wondered if those books would ever be used again.

Two tiny bedrooms, jutting out on either side of the hall, made the house look spacious from the front. It definitely was not. The only sitting area was in a corner of the kitchen.

Months ago, men claiming to be bushwhackers showed up and took a fancy to the bed frames, feather mattresses, and all the covers in the loft. Ma said there was no telling who they really were. She suspected they were Kansans on account of them taking furniture. Those guys were famous for hauling furniture across the state line to sell.

"If only they'd left the pillows," Joshua complained.

"Aw, we can live without pillows. Problem is your head's too hard," Grandpa teased.

Joshua's deadpan look of disgust made the old fellow roar with laughter. "At least, they didn't steal my sign," he said. "Guess none of 'em needed it, beings their name ain't Homer Carter." The sign was a personalized gift from Cyrus, back in 1860, for Homer's fifty-fifth birthday, just months before the rebellion began. What fun the boys had showing all the neighbors!

Suddenly, as if on cue, a beam of moonlight came through

the tiny windowpane overlooking the front yard. It fell onto the sign above Grandpa's head, making Joshua laugh once again.

Here lies Homer Carter.
May he rest in peace
With no snoring.

"You are so-o-o fortunate, Joshua," Pa would say if he were around at this very moment. No matter the losses, Pa insisted on looking at what remained. Generally, it irked Joshua. Yet, tonight, it was what he needed to hear.

So he began a monologue, speaking softly to himself, imagining what else his father might say. "You have two older men left in your life plus a wonderful mother. Nobody can take away your memories. There will be good times ahead..... patience, my boy."

Pa should be home, helping make all the decisions. He should be there to protect his wife and children who were missing him terribly. Yet Joshua knew what Pa would say about that, too: "Remember, son. 'Should be's' are like luxuries—nice to have, but not essential."

Perhaps it was the distant gunshots from minutes ago, maybe Grandpa's snoring, the heat, or all three together. Whatever, he was too restless to stay inside.

So about two hours past midnight, with legs dangling off the edge of the old, rotten back porch, he stared into the dark, thinking about the day he and Andrew met.

Andrew was eleven, Joshua only seven, when Uncle John pulled up to their place with a wagon load of wares. As a skilled tinsmith, the man peddled everything from pots and pans to pill boxes and candle holders. In an attempt to expand his business, he made trips a little further west to Hickman Mills, circling back to Big Cedar and Hargis Store, a few miles east of the Carter place. Andrew always went along to keep his uncle company.

"We've come to check out fishing holes," Uncle John announced as soon as he'd said hello.

"The best fishing hole I know is about 200 feet from here." Cyrus declared, pointing toward the Little Blue River.

"It's quite a distance for you to come, but you're welcome anytime," Ma told the guests a few hours later, as they feasted on blue gill and catfish. "In fact, if you like, drop Andrew off while you make your rounds, John."

Uncle John could never have guessed what good friends the boys would soon become. Neither would he know how much Joshua would come to look up to Andrew, who, like Joshua, was known as "big brother" in his own rapidly-growing family.

Back in the beginning, nobody could predict that the peaceful Little Blue River would grow to such a popular hiding place for bushwhackers either. Yet, in the interim, the boys had many wonderful times together.

The two would squeeze into the loft and talk until midnight. Next morning they'd get up early and dash out to the river when fishing was at its best.

Once the war began, Andrew's trips were few and far between; and they seldom got down to the fishing hole. Ma wanted them to stay close to the house. So they talked mostly about old times and all of the ordinary things they missed, like going to well-stocked stores each Saturday.

Pa wouldn't have been happy with them discussing politics. That was one subject off limits for his children. It probably was the same with most parents. Joshua figured it was more so in their household, considering the unpopular views the Carter kids might overhear. So he was left to wonder how his friend felt about many things that mattered a lot in the Carter family.

Since Andrew's grandfather owned slaves, there was a

good chance the family was Confederate. At first it was hard to know, though. For some Unionists in western Missouri were slaveholders, too. Yet many Confederates were not, though they saw nothing wrong with what was sometimes referred to as "the peculiar institution." Unionists simply were against splitting the nation into two separate countries, while Secessionists-- Confederates, that is--were fighting for that privilege.

The question was settled in late April of 1862, the same morning that Joshua noticed the signs of the white oak coming back to life after a long winter. Uncle John stopped by with the sad news that he and Andrew wouldn't be coming at all for a while. They would be taking up the slack left by Andrew's father, who had recently left for Arkansas to fight with the Confederacy.

Now, as he sat grieving, there were things Joshua wondered about the Owsleys that he'd never cared to know before. Did they live in a big house or one even tinier than the Carter's? Did Andrew still fight with his younger brother as much as Joshua did with Billy or had they grown closer as they'd grown older? Crazy—how he longed to know such things now when the hope of inquiring was gone.

"Andrew Owsley is like the big brother Joshua never knew." Ma always had a faraway look in her eyes when she spoke of Richard, born in Tennessee, same year as Andrew. At three, Richard died of typhoid fever, a year after his stillborn baby sister named Margaret and only a year before Joshua came along.

The sadness made Pa restless. "We needed a new start," he always said. "It was bad enough surrounded by so many poor, suffering souls in slavery, often separated from loved ones by the cruel system. We hated that. Then, after losing our only two children, everything we touched reminded us of sorrow. It all seemed to mingle together. At first, I took off west in search of gold … stopped when I got to Missouri and saw the rich farmland, so abundant and almost free to settlers. It looked better than gold to me, so I staked my claim and went back for Pa and Lucy."

In a few hours, Joshua would be leaving behind everything that reminded him of Andrew. Maybe leaving would help erase his sorrow. Yet he wasn't sure if his parents had gotten away from theirs or simply traded one set of troubles for another.

By the time he was nine, Ma had frequently pled to leave Missouri like so many of their Unionist neighbors had while Pa insisted on staying with his land. Odd—though neither would have chosen this outcome, both seemed to be getting their way.

To learn what it might have been like to live through the terrifying experience of guerrilla warfare for years on end, go to:

http://www.sos.mo.gov/mdh/DividedLoyalties/dl_atour_media.asp?dl=p29

4

"Don't try to push the memories out of your mind," Cyrus Carter told his son whenever either of them mentioned last year's Battle of Lone Jack. "If you do, you'll lose the good ones along with the bad."

Every time he thought of the horror of that sweltering August day, Joshua felt closer to Andrew. Yet, with travel plans now changing, he was a little relieved. Even before yesterday's shooting, the thought of going back through Lone Jack, seeing all the reminders, made him quite anxious.

Most Lone Jack citizens fled town as soon as they heard

the cannon fire the night before the battle. With the boom loud enough to carry as far west as Hargis Store, news soon reached the Carters.

Cyrus had the opposite reaction. He was going. Despite being a wanted man because of refusing to sign up for the Missouri State Militia as required by Governor Gamble, he would risk his life if he thought he could help anyone. Homer was going, too. If anything happened to his son, he planned to be right beside him.

Lucy wasn't happy. She and Cyrus argued most of the night. Not only did he insist on going himself. He wanted to take Joshua with him, saying the boy was old enough to see and learn from war firsthand. As usual, Lucy gave in, much to the joy of her son, who couldn't appreciate his mother's tears when they left before next morning's sunrise.

They traveled three hours, arriving in Lone Jack soon after the shooting ceased. Still in the wagon, staring at the grizzly scene, Joshua sort of wished his mother had won last night's argument. His stomach turned at the sight and smell of blood and guts. Hardest were the outcries from wounded teenagers. He felt helpless and sad. The sight of over one-hundred horses, dead in a river of blood, upset him as much as the soldiers lying among them, many who had used the horses as shields. Scores of other corpses lay near ditch diggers, a hundred yards from where Pa stopped.

"What an odd battle!" people were saying. Unlike most, it occurred in the middle of town as bystanders watched friends and relatives fight at close range. Much was hand-to-hand combat, since many newly-enlisted Confederate men had yet to be issued guns.

As Grandpa tethered their own horses, Joshua heard a familiar voice calling his name over the groans of the wounded. It was Andrew, sitting in the street beside a soldier in blue.

Both looked forlorn. The wounded man, his ghastly white head rolling side to side, cried out for water. A few of his guts lay on top his belly. Joshua turned aside, almost losing the sandwich he'd devoured an hour earlier.

"It's my cousin," Andrew explained. "William Dyer from Lexington."

"Hi, William," Grandpa spoke tenderly, kneeling beside the young soldier. Steadying himself, Joshua moved closer, too. He knelt just behind Grandpa.

From the looks of things, William and Andrew were on opposite sides of the conflict like many families. Even brothers sometimes fought against one another. Yet Joshua knew Andrew well enough to be certain it would make no difference.

Andrew turned to Cyrus, standing at Dyer's feet. "I got the blood stopped, Mr. Carter. Doctors are trying hard, but not getting to everyone in time--just too many needing attention."

Cyrus located water and some cotton wool. Gently, he cared for William while listening to Andrew tell how he'd seen scores of men fall that morning from a concealed vantage point behind a building. From there, he watched the two huge cannons rolling back and forth across the street as each army fought to gain control of them.

At one point, he slipped inside to escape the horrors, but failed. "The shots inside were like the sound of popcorn, hitting the lid of a big, hot skillet. Problem is I was inside the skillet… felt lucky to get out of there!" he exclaimed. "This is the last battle I want to ever see." he said, hanging his head.

"Me too, Andrew… Me too," Grandpa agreed, putting his arm across the young man's shoulders.

"Is this George Manning?" asked Cyrus, now leaning over a fellow in grey with a gaping head wound, lying near William.

Andrew turned to see. "Yes, it is," he half whispered. "I don't

18

think he's gonna make it." Manning wasn't seeing a thing. His eyes, wide open, were glazed over.

"I see Dr. Cundiff near the hotel," Cyrus said, now standing, wiping his own brow. "I'll ask his advice. We need to get these men out of this scorching heat."

Joshua knew lots of stories about the good doctor. Not long ago bushwhackers had blindfolded him and took him for a long ride to a cabin where ole' Quantrill lay injured. They removed the blindfold long enough for the doc to sew the wounds up, then replaced it and took him home.

Dr. Cundiff was a Unionist, but today he and two of his colleagues bound wounds for both sides. The misery made equals of everyone.

Soon Pa was back. "Give me a hand, Joshua. We're going to prepare a bed for these two in the wagon." As they worked, he quietly explained the plan. "Dr. Cundiff has been forced to make many difficult decisions today. While it may sound cruel, in a situation with this many casualties, it's sometimes necessary to leave the most critical to die rather than risk losing many others more likely to be saved. The good doc doesn't think either one of them has a chance, but he's gonna soon try to stitch Dyer up, at least. Says it can't do any harm for us to take them back to our place and do what we can to keep them comfortable.

"I expect Lucy could send for the medicine woman she knows, and maybe Sam and Olivia will let us use their spare room and help us take care of them," Grandpa said.

Andrew agreed to get word to the families about where they might find the two wounded men.

Pa handed Joshua a bottle of whiskey. "Dr. Cundiff says just give 'em a few sips now and then if they wake up and start to complain."

Joshua nodded. He climbed in and arranged the quilts to

make a soft cushion for himself between the soldiers. Once settled, he glanced again at the trenches.

"Pa, look, it's Rev. Miller!" he cried.

Suddenly a fellow with a big bottle of whiskey shoved the minister away from a corpse in blue. "Leave them be," the assailant shouted. "Union guys don't even deserve a burial."

"Stay with the wounded, Joshua," Cyrus said. He and Grandpa dashed off to intervene. Another man, closer to the troublemaker, beat them to it. The fellow with the bottle soon nursed a small knot on his head while the minister continued digging.

It had been months since they'd seen their Presbyterian pastor. With Pa in hiding and it too dangerous for families to be on the road, none of the Carters had gotten down to Pleasant Hill for the monthly dinner-on-the ground and all-day-singing meetings since March. Oh, how they'd missed it!

"Looks like I'm not the only father fool enough to bring a boy to the battlefield," Joshua overheard Pa say as he shook hands with Mr. Henley. Though a staunch Confederate, Henley and his young son were loading a Union soldier with a serious leg wound into a wagon.

"I know this man's family," Henley declared. "He's two days from home, but our home will be his until he's well enough to travel."

Odd how many at Lone Jack had quickly gone from being friends to enemies, then back again, thought Joshua.

"Who won?" he asked Andrew as they prepared to go their separate ways. Until that moment, it hadn't mattered. He wasn't sure it did now.

"Some say the Confederates won," Andrew replied. "At least, the Union ran out of ammunition first. If you ask me, I don't think anybody won." He extended his arm toward the street with a wide arc. "There were lots of brave men here, Joshua, but not a winner among them as I see it. If so, what did they win?" Both boys hung their heads in grief.

Joshua gave each man a shot of whiskey and waved to his good friend, never thinking that this might be the last time they'd ever be together.

5

Not only did the men survive. They became good friends while lying in the same room recovering. Never mind that one was a Unionist, the other a Confederate.

Joshua was thrilled to ride with his father to return the two to their families in late October, but he was saddened at what his father told him on the way home.

"I'm going to visit my good friend John Wornall again in Westport in a few weeks. I could end up staying a couple of months, just to get me through the worst of the winter. Hiding out in the warmer months is hard enough, but it's miserable when a guy can't get warm. John told me last time I was there that I was welcome to come for an extended stay if I ever should feel the need. I know you'll do your best to help take care of things around here."

Joshua knew it did his father good to visit Mr. Wornall. He could understand why, too. He'd met the kind man himself on one occasion. He hadn't minded his father going to Westport before now. He always came home with exciting things—books, magazines, stories, new ideas. Yet it would be harder this time to have him away with things more tense than ever.

Things settled down a lot that winter, though. It was like all the guerrillas must have been hiding out, too. And there weren't any serious battles around like they'd seen at Lone Jack or had heard of elsewhere in the area.

As usual, when Pa did get back in late February, he had a fresh, new story to tell. This one he'd read in the *Daily Journal of Commerce* while at Westport. It was about Cole Younger. "You remember him, don't you, Joshua? ... the son of Henry Younger?"

He didn't remember at first. Pa patiently explained. "Henry was the mayor of Harrisonville, used to stop by to see us and ask me to go to Kansas City with him. Remember?"

"Oh, yes, of course, and you were always eager to go along," Joshua replied. "Wasn't he murdered this summer?"

"Yes ... and on a trip to Kansas City, too. Fortunately, I wasn't along that time. Cole, quickly concluded that the killer was a Unionist. Yet what he did would have grieved Henry immensely. That lad took off and joined William Quantrill's gang. Seems he was full of rage and out to hurt anybody who might get in his way, as if revenge could bring his father back. I wish I'd had a chance to talk to Cole, think I could have comforted him, helped him make better decisions."

The story the newspaper carried was also about Union Major Emory Foster and his brother, who were both wounded and lying in a building that day at Lone Jack. Suddenly, an angry Confederate approached the two brothers and drew his gun. At that very instant, however, Cole Younger walked in, saw what was happening, and threw the gunman out, declaring Foster a friend of his family.

Moments later, Foster called Cole over, thanked him for saving their lives, and gave him some money along with a message he wanted to send to his mother. Cole agreed to deliver both.

Foster soon recovered. When he went to see his mother, she had every cent. To Pa, the story offered hope that even the bitterest of men in this war could have a change of heart in time.

"Do you think Cole will ever go back to being the same person he was before his father was killed?" Joshua asked.

"No, not the same person, though he could end up being a stronger, kinder man in the end. I think it could go either way. It just depends on how Cole might want the rest of his story to be written."

Soon Pa returned to his secret hiding place, never coming back home without an exchange of chickadee calls with his son, indicating all was fine for Cyrus to come out of hiding. Twice this summer, Joshua had summoned his father with a signal of distress. The first was in early July when a letter arrived from Andrew. His father was dead! It had taken six weeks for the family to get the news from Vicksburg, where Mr. Owsley had been shot down in early May. It was up to Andrew now to take on the responsibility of raising his five younger siblings. Never had Joshua needed his own father more than that day, and he came quickly and stayed until late in the night. Joshua's heart was torn in two with an anguish that had not been surpassed until yesterday with the news of Andrew's death.

The other summons had gone out as soon as they got word of the Lawrence massacre. Now, as he sat on the old, rotten, back porch, he thought of Pa. Then, he thought of Andrew. He wasn't sure how much he wanted to be like either one. Both had taken risks to help others, but look where it had gotten them. Was it worth it? Fighting was one way of taking a risk. So was refusing to fight, as Pa had done. Joshua wasn't sure he'd have the courage to do either.

Facing the task of tomorrow morning was hard enough to think about. Looking out toward the river, he shuddered. Pa was counting on him. The whole family was. If he messed up, they might never get to Iowa.

6

Inside he found Grandpa staring out the east window of the kitchen. The flames from burning houses lit up the horizon as bright as day. "Looks like all the demons on Earth have died and come back to life, bringing hell-fire right here to Jackson County," the old man said as Joshua came near to stand by his grandfather's side.

The boy drew closer. He felt his Grandpa's gnarled hand touch his shoulder. "When will the revenge ever stop?" Grandpa wondered aloud. That was anyone's guess, but Joshua hoped his grandfather, with the benefit of so many years, might answer a question that had been running through his own mind for hours.

"Grandpa, why would they go after someone like Andrew?"

"There's no good reason," Grandpa replied. "They shoot first and ask questions later." He reached out and pulled the boy even closer. "Word is that some of Andrew's family helped feed Quantrill's men on the way to Lawrence. Even if they did, it doesn't mean they had a choice, though. Any family who's tried *not* feeding Quantrill's gang knows how risky that can be."

"Imagine something like this happening, anywhere in the land of the free." Joshua said. "Seems nobody around here is safe these days."

"Well, at least one part of 'The Star-Spangled Banner' applies to folks along our borders," said Grandpa. "Though the United States has never really been 'a land of the free' for everyone, this whole area is indeed 'the home of the brave.'"

"The home of the bravest if you're counting men like Pa and Andrew Owsley," Joshua returned.

"Don't forget slaves running for their lives. Or your mama, child. Nor boys who get stubborn mules down hot, dusty roads."

24

Joshua smiled faintly as he fought back tears and struggled to speak. "Or an old man who sticks by his family no matter what," he whispered in his grandpa's ear. "I love you, Grandpa."

"I love you, too," the response came. They sat in silence a good ten minutes before Grandpa recovered his voice. "It all reminds me of the Trail of Tears," he said.

Glancing sideways, Joshua noticed the old man's wet, leathery cheeks. He knew exactly what was next. He'd heard the words a hundred times before.

"1838—'twas the first time I'd realized how unfair life could be, depending on the color of a person's skin. So many downtrodden souls passed by our property."

Though half Cherokee himself, Grandpa avoided being on that trail only because of his white mother, who was from a prominent family.

"Grandpa, is the war now causing a new set of problems for those in Indian Territory?" Joshua asked.

Grandpa had no way of knowing, but he was quick to point out the big differences between Order No. 11 and the Trail of Tears. "Granted, the sorrows and suffering in both stories are mighty big," he admitted. "Yet most of us being forced to leave our Missouri homes are of the same race as those in power. And unlike with the Trail of Tears, many of us may return home someday."

"Do you think we'll be among those returning?" Joshua asked.

"Hard to say, but I know one thing. Wherever we end up and no matter which side of this rebellion wins, I intend to be among the winners."

"That's what Pa said a few days before he left for Lawrence," Joshua said.

"Yes, I well remember—was it something about the winners of a war being those who come out caring more about others than ever before?"

"Yes Grandpa," Joshua whispered. "That's exactly what he said." He gently encircled his grandfather's neck from behind. "Isn't it about two hours before sunrise?"

Grandpa nodded.

Up in the loft, Joshua was soon fast asleep despite sounds from beneath the "tombstone" that reverberated across the small space at a volume nearing that of an approaching tornado.

*****

"If Lucy'd managed to get that old red rooster cooked last night, like she planned to do, I might be sleeping 'til noon today," Grandpa said, stretching his arms. He groaned loudly, looking at the rafters just above his head. "Instead the old cock is crowing right on schedule, right up to our last day. "

Joshua sprang to a sitting position, crossing his clenched fists over his chest, panting. "It was just a dream," he whispered to himself a moment later as his hands moved in reflex to his neck, ascertaining that he wasn't being choked by anyone except the ghost in his imagination. He felt silly. After all, the nightmare had been about such a simple task that now lay before him. Yet the simplest could become extremely complicated in light of recent challenges. Ignoring that fact, he jumped up and reached for his shirt.

Watching his grandpa climb down the ladder in response to some routine call for help from Jenny, he realized how much he wanted to make the old man proud. Despite the difference in years, he longed to be equal in courage and strength, though he knew he couldn't come close to the wisdom gained from years of experience.

Did courage come faster if a guy pretended everything was normal? It just might.

"I am the strong one, the confident one," he told himself, which was what he'd often heard his parents say about him. To be honest, he found it difficult to see himself as strong, knowing that a boy's courage and strength were measured in western Missouri differently than what he'd been taught. Being different was hard for a boy. It was all so confusing.

He wondered if the war would be over before he'd have it all figured out. Could he prove himself without going off to fight? How would his old friends feel about him if they should someday meet again after the war?

His mother's words from last night now rose above everything. "Before first light, get out to the white oak," she'd reminded him, just before he climbed into the loft. "Dig down and find what your father has left for us. Don't forget to leave the note. It may be our only hope of him finding us." She paused. "And please, Joshua.....all the while you must watch for strangers." Her warnings made him feel like a child.

"Yes, Ma," he respectfully replied. "I know."

How could he possibly forget? His parents had reminded him of the emergency plan many times over the last six months.

Being the oldest living son was sometimes a privilege but often an enormous burden. Just like now … if Richard was alive. Truth is if he was, he might soon be dead—same as Andrew. No use thinking about what might have been. He had a job to do, might as well get it over with.

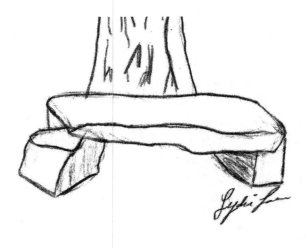

7

To both Cyrus and Joshua, the stones under the white oak tree served as a special place where the two could talk about weighty matters or just share a laugh on good days. There they'd take time to notice a storm rolling in or tell a story about adventures in the woods. Sometimes, in one breath talking about bringing home a mess of fish while speaking of the nation's problems in the next. Joshua didn't pretend to understand as much as Cyrus did, but he hoped to someday. So he listened, trying to make sense of what seemed so senseless.

He figured he'd learned about as much while sitting on those stones as he had sitting on a school bench. In fact, it was hard to separate one experience from the other. Pa had served a dual role, as both father and teacher until Ma had been forced into that role with lessons being held at the kitchen table this past year.

With his father forced to hide out more and more frequently, the brief times under the tree became really precious. Joshua didn't ever know just where to find his father. It would have been too dangerous for both if he had. He did know about the manmade cave, though he'd never seen it. From there, Pa was able to hear Joshua's special "bird call" that served as a signal for him to stay hidden if danger was near.

Joshua often wondered if Billy was jealous. Surely he would have noticed how often his older brother and father carried on private conversations. If he cared, though, he never let on.

Just days after Pa returned from Westport, Joshua learned of the extra-special place *beneath* the stones. For years, his parents had stashed away a little money, every time they could. It wasn't much, Cyrus told his son. But it was the only "bank" the family had, and the only place Cyrus could think of as a reliable spot for leaving hidden messages in the event the family might somehow get separated. At first, Joshua couldn't imagine this. Then, as more and more people had stories to tell and more skeletons were found, he began to realize his father's plan might be important someday.

He stepped off the old, rotten stoop and reached for the shovel, thinking back to that initial conversation.

"Buried treasure?" he remembered asking. "We have buried treasure right here?"

Pa snickered. And, thinking back now, Joshua laughed at the reply. "Well, sort of, though I'm not sure it's enough to call it 'treasure.' Hopefully, there's enough to get the family to a safer place if need be. In war things can happen quickly, son. Let's just call what's below us the 'just-in-case money.' In fact, buddy, it's *inside a case* of sorts…actually a tin. So here's what you do…."

It was time to get moving. Yet all he could think of, standing near the back door, were last night's gunshots on top of yesterday's awful news. Pushing those thoughts aside, he slowly took in everything between the house and the barn, where their two lone milk cows and Old Nelly waited. Everything looked undisturbed. He turned toward the corn crib and empty chicken coop. At least there were no eggs to gather today. Two days ago, they'd feasted on the last chicken, and the only eggs they'd have for three weeks were now inside the flour barrel packed in the cart already.

He slowly walked out about twenty feet before stopping. The grass by the white oak stood tall, no breezes stirring. He stopped to listen to the mourning doves. He'd never before understood their funny name. For, until now, they'd never sounded sad. In fact, they generally served as a comforting reminder that a new day with possibilities of discovery lay ahead. Suddenly, anything he could think about discovering on the trip ahead brought the opposite feelings of days past. Were there mourning doves in Iowa? He hoped so.

Those silly birds had reason to sing today, more than ever. After all, they were free and would stay in their natural homes, not needing to ask questions about anything. Their soft cooing would keep filling the air above the consuming fires, even if nobody heard them.

He longed just to make time stand still, to stay right in this spot, to have Pa come riding up, saying it was all a mistake, calling for life to return to normal. "Come on, Josh. Grab a pole. Let's go fishing. Everything of the last two weeks was just a nightmare like the one at daybreak."

That was just the daydream he needed. Soon, as if his father was watching his every move, he sprinted toward the tree, ready to have this job finished, no matter what happened next. Moments later, he leaned his shovel against the tree trunk and stopped long enough to look around and catch his breath. He half expected to see the giant, muscular guy from his latest nightmare suddenly step from the tall, undisturbed corn. It was eerily quiet. Even the mourning doves had stopped cooing. After moving the large stone aside, he reached for the two smaller ones that served as legs for the makeshift seat, thinking how nice it would be to find flat stones like these for another bench in Iowa. Yet with neither Pa nor Andrew around to share it, what purpose would it serve? Somehow, it seemed odd to think of sitting alone under a tree, even with important matters to contemplate. A stone bench, in his experience, was always for two.

Coming out of his daydream, he reached for the shovel and thrust it into the parched earth, bringing up a dry clod no larger than his fist. Why should he expect more after weeks without a drop of rain? He went for another try ..... and froze!

Somebody was in the tall prairie grass to the east of the cornfield, slowly coming his way. Could it be two? Maybe a half dozen, he decided, after listening closer. He dared not look up. Wishing to be invisible, he eased the shovel down quietly and sank to the ground, shoulders shrugged, arms wrapped tightly across his chest, hands toward the back, elbows touching, ankles crossed, and knees drawn up under his chin, he drew in all the oxygen he could--and held it. Uncontrollable trembling started at his jaw and continued all the way to his ankles. Whoever was there need not ask what he was digging. They'd already know. With banks both inconvenient and untrustworthy, rural people commonly hid money in the ground.

The family needed whatever they'd saved to get resettled. It was money they'd worked hard for. With what little extra farm produce there'd been since the war started, most cash came from Ma's sewing and egg sales. To think of being robbed made his blood boil, yet he was frustrated by his sense of helplessness, making him angrier than ever.

As with most nineteenth-century boys, viewed more like men than children by the time they were ten years old, anger was okay—as long as it was anger at something threatening the family. Boys were supposed to be ready to fight like a man, even if—no, especially if—they were needed for war. Well, he was strong and would help care for his family, too, even if it killed him.

The noise suddenly stopped. Maybe they hadn't seen him, after all. Or maybe they were just waiting, hoping he'd get up and start digging again so they wouldn't have to do a thing until what they wanted was in his hands. Then, they'd be off and running, carrying away all hope.

The swishing started again, this time several feet closer. When finally forced to exhale, he made more noise than he'd intended. Slowly and quietly he drew in an ample supply of oxygen and waited until, much to his embarrassment, he felt tears running down his cheeks. Oh, how he hated to be seen crying!

What were those thieves doing now? Silence, but not for long…. Suddenly, there were sounds of something rushing toward him. ….. His cheeks were really wet now. What a strange sensation! It felt like having a gentle face-wash. ….. His eyes popped open as he burst into spontaneous laughter.

"Hey, Fox!" he cried. Behind his old red hound stood Skipper and Rufus, the Mullin's cocker spaniels. Joshua hugged all three at once. "You guys want to go treasure hunting?" he asked, laughing and rolling with them on the ground.

Soon he was digging again, and didn't stop until he reached the old tobacco tin, exactly where Pa said it would be. Inside were three wads of money. Not wanting to risk counting it in the open, he quickly stuffed a wad in each pants pocket and the third into the pocket of his shirt before checking one last time the note he'd written for his father.

"Headed to Salem, Iowa, with the Mullins. Hope to see you soon. Love, Josh."

What else was there to say? Tucking the message inside the tin, he secured the lid, reached for the shovel, and suddenly stopped to question himself. What was this piece of shiny, red metal with a green corner that protruded up toward him? Was it important? If so, why had Pa never mentioned it?

Now, on all fours, his hands worked eagerly. He chuckled at Fox, moving his own paws just as frantically as if he smelled a meaty bone below, rather than running off to play with the two cocker spaniels. Soon they unearthed a tin box, about two inches thick, ten inches long, and six wide. He grasped it with both hands and stared in wonder. Leaning against the tree, he pried it open to find pages and pages of notes in his father's hand-writing, some dating back to 1861. Interspersed were newspaper clippings and magazine articles.

He unfolded the top note, dated August 17, 1863. "All we can do now is live for peace," he read in a whisper. Laying the page against his chest, he tenderly caressed it and breathed a silent prayer. These words, written just five days before Pa left for Lawrence, he sensed he would treasure for a long time to come.

Was this how his father kept his mind occupied during the long days of hiding in the woods? Would he be happy to find his son had taken these things that weren't really his to take? Joshua could only guess. Carefully, he dusted off the box and set it near the stones before covering the hole.

Next, he rebuilt the bench, then dusted off his hands and stood back to admire his accomplishment. If only Pa would soon find his way back home, these stones would be in place and the message waiting for him.

He swelled with pride as he started toward the house with shovel in hand. Halfway to the back porch, it dawned on him that he'd totally forgotten his ordinary routine. Every morning he fed and watered the animals without fail, milking the cows, too—all before breakfast. How could he have so easily forgotten?

Back on track, he soon had the pail of warm milk in one hand, the treasure box in the other, as he strolled out of the barn. He was starving, but he must stop for one last routine— this one at the smallest structure on the property.

8

Inside the weather-beaten outhouse, he laid the treasure box atop the closed seat to his left, raised the lid on the seat nearest the door, and made himself comfortable. As soon as breakfast was over, he'd finish loading the cart and they'd be on the road.

Seconds later, reaching to unlatch the door, he stopped in midair. Strange male voices only a few feet away! What was going on out there? Listening closer, he heard another voice—his mother's. She sounded frantic as she desperately tried to reason with the two intruders.

He leaned forward, careful not to make a sound, closed one eye, and peered through the knothole a few inches below the latch. Ma held Baby George close to her heart, though it did nothing to lessen his ear-splitting screams as the baby searched her terrified face for some sign of comfort.

Had these men been watching him under the tree? Did they know he was in the outhouse now? Had Ma seen them from indoors and come out to investigate? Or maybe she'd been out back of the barn, already loading the cart. He closed one eye to get a better look, held his breath, and listened closely.

"We don't have anything left!" Lucy cried in a high-pitched voice. "Four men came by two days ago and got the rest of our bedding, even most of my children's clothes."

"What about horses?" a stocky man asked. "You got to ride out of here on something."

"We have an old, stubborn mule," Ma replied impatiently. "He'll be pulling a cart. It's only big enough for two small children to ride on top of what little we have left to take."

"Well, Horace," the skinny guy said, raising his eyebrow and smirking. "I think we could *use* an old mule."

Horace smiled agreeably.

Joshua gasped. How he longed to run to the rescue! Instead, he wisely remembered his father's reminders to stay put. "Oddly enough," Pa explained, "white women are seldom in danger in this day of chivalry. Even in the presence of guerrillas, they are usually protected almost like gods. We men and older boys are the ones likely to get hurt, especially if another guy feels threatened. So stay out of the way as much as possible, Joshua,

35

and the whole family will have a better chance of staying safe."

Besides, Joshua had treasures to protect, he told himself. Not just money; but precious papers yet to be examined. There was no telling what his father might have written or put away for future reference. The fact he'd chosen to hide it made Joshua uneasy, unsure whether the contents might incense one group of ruffians or another, if not the Union army itself.

The hairs on the back of his neck stood straight up. What if the men got close enough to see his eye through the knothole? Could they possibly have heard him gasp just now? Backing away, he sat on the closed toilet seat, looking around in desperation before spying a crack just above his left elbow. Useless, he concluded, since it only gave him a view of the kitchen door.

As if sent to prove him wrong at that very instant, Grandpa stepped outside and off the porch. Joshua covered his mouth and worked hard not to laugh out loud at the walking stick he leaned on. It was an old hickory cane long forgotten—one his father made for his own use after spraining his ankle years ago. Where did Grandpa even find it?

Hobbling toward the visitors, the "cripple" looked like a pathetic, stooped-over, harmless eighty-year-old. He walked ever so slowly, taking tiny steps, grimacing as if in great pain. "Good thinking, Grandpa," Joshua whispered. "You don't look the least bit threatening."

The disguise was remarkable! Chances are these men had never seen him before. Even if they had, they'd never recognize him now. Good thing they didn't know how strong this white-headed fellow was. Joshua smiled, daring to peer once again through the big knothole.

If Grandpa hadn't been so able-bodied, Pa might have considered filing for a hardship exemption on the new draft orders, just before the Lawrence raid. Having an elderly parent in need of care was one way to avoid joining up. "They'd take one look at my father and fit both of us for a uniform," Cyrus had joked.

Finally reaching the visitors, Grandpa's confident voice commanded respect. What is it you need, soldiers?" he inquired, extending his hand politely to each man. How smooth of him, pretending these guys were really soldiers! "I'm the man in charge around here now 'cause my son is over in Lawrence helping his sister and others rebuild."

"Is that so?" said the stocky guy. "Well, I'm from Lawrence. So what's your daughter's name?"

What difference should that make? With Lawrence nearly half the size of Kansas City, chances were slim this fellow would know Aunt Charlotte. He must be trying to just catch the old cripple off guard.

"Charlotte Potter," Grandpa answered, matter-of-factly. "Her husband's Simpson."

"Simpson Potter!" the visitor exclaimed. "Why Simpson is one of my neighbors! My young'uns play with his young'uns. Why, yes! Come to think of it, I think I met your son. Name Cyrus?" he asked. Grandpa nodded.

"I never would have thought about a Missourian being over there helping out abolitionists," the stocky man declared.

"Yes, indeed. Cyrus is my son, and I'm proud of him. We plan to meet up with him on our way north."

"So when you leaving?" asked the skinny guest.

"Planned to be on the road by 6 o'clock... looks like we may not make it," replied Lucy.

"Well, don't let *us* stop you," Horace returned. "We wouldn't want to keep you from following orders. Have a safe journey, now."

The skinny man waved at Jenny, Tom, and Billy, all peeking out from the west window. At last, they were leaving. Grandpa cautiously limped off, slowly as he'd come, just in case they happened to turn around.

Where was Ma? Taking the front entrance? Finally, concluding it safe, Joshua flung the toilet door open, and bumped straight into her.

She gasped. "Where did you come from, Joshua Carter? And what on earth do you have in your hands?"

He spoke softly, like someone with a great secret, as he gazed into his mother's eyes. "Treasures we could have lost before getting a chance to ever see them," he replied.

Handing her the tin box, he patted all three pockets for reassurance. "I was just thinking. It's a good thing nature called me to the toilet when it did."

Grandpa leaned his cane against the outhouse, gave Joshua a bear hug, and reached for the fresh pail of milk a few feet away. "And I was just thinking, it's a good thing nature didn't call *anyone else* to join you while you waited."

"Come on in this house, you two," said Ma, joining their laughter. She gave the tin back to Joshua and put an arm around his shoulder. Balanced on her hip, Baby George squealed with delight.

9

Lucy quickly shifted her attention to the children waiting inside. She handed the baby to Joshua, immediately enveloping the other three in her outstretched arms as she knelt to look each child in the face before turning to the next.

"Good morning," she said with a comforting smile. "This is moving day. Do you have everything ready to go?"

"Lizzy and I do," Jenny answered eagerly. She pulled her rag doll from the soft bundle made by the tattered, pink blanket. No need to worry about Jenny—she'd have her two most prized possessions ready at any hour of the day, never parted with either.

"The Mullins family will be over soon. When they arrive, we should be ready to go," Lucy told them. At that point, she shifted into her usual morning reminders. "Tom, put the plates around. Jenny, get the forks and spoons. Billy, out to the pump--one bucket of water on the porch, the other inside."

By the time Billy returned, Joshua had a plate piled high with hardtack. Normally, he would have been stacking Ma's wonderful biscuits, fresh out of the oven. There was no time for baking biscuits this morning, though. She had other things to do and so did Billy and Tom, who normally took turns beating the dough for a half hour with the hammer each morning to make the biscuits more tender and tasty.

"Good thing we made plenty of sheet iron last week," Grandpa joked. Others referred to hardtack as "tooth dullers." Grandpa always claimed "sheet iron" was the best description for the hard crackers. They were especially popular for soldier rations since they packed easily and could be stored for long periods of time. Soldiers sometimes found invaders sharing their snacks, however, so they liked to call them "worm castles." On the trip ahead, the Carters and Mullins would be surviving on hardtack, just like the soldiers, grateful for anything they could get to go with it.

Lucy reached into a barrel near the back door and took out a hunk of salt pork, dripping in brine. From the size of it, Joshua knew she was making an extra-large pan of gravy. They'd need it. There'd be more hardtack and a few pieces of dried apple when they stopped to rest in the midday heat, but nothing more until supper.

Still bouncing the baby on his side, he extracted the three wads of money from his pockets, laying it on the little counter where his mother was working. It was more cash than he'd ever seen in one place. To his disappointment, without even counting it, Ma immediately scooped it up, tightly packing it in the little drawstring purse. He knew better than to ask questions. His parents never talked about money in front of the children.

However, when she'd pulled the bag out just yesterday, he couldn't help noticing how limp it was. Already, the children had been warned not to expect anything beyond the basics for a long time to come, though Ma was confident they would eventually find living easier once away from the constant turmoil of western Missouri.

"Thank you, Son. This will be a big help." Lucy placed the bag atop the tin box. Apparently, she noticed the question in his eyes. "It's enough," she said, with an assuring nod.

Enough? Enough for *what*? To keep them from starving-- provided they weren't robbed in the meantime? Enough to buy a good horse and everything they would need to replace? Even if he knew the dollar amount today, it was impossible to predict from one day to the next what prices might be even in Jackson County, let alone Iowa. Nothing was certain, between inflation and shortages, both worse the further south one went.

With the steaming breakfast on the table, Billy and Tom took their usual places on a long, backless bench against the wall, leaving just enough room for Joshua on the other side, next to Jenny. Like most three-year-olds, she needed supervision to see she got fed and cleaned up. With Pa gone, this was another of Joshua's assignments. Homer and Lucy each took an end.

Grandpa reached for Joshua's hand, then stretched to take his daughter-in-law's as she strained to meet his in the middle. What came next was the longest prayer Joshua ever remembered. He kept opening one eye to glance at the gravy, as if doing so would keep it hot 'til Grandpa finished.

"Thank you, God, for the bounty here. No matter which way we go, sustain us and all our neighbors moving one way or t'other. May Cyrus know peace today....and all those in Lawrence." His voice choked with tears. "Thanks, most of all, for Andrew Owsley. He brought much joy into our lives." He paused. "Now, God, bless his family. Give them strength to carry on." He took a deep breath, but not to say "Amen." A collective sigh rose from the children, except for Baby George. He wasn't the least concerned about anything except crawling on top of the table to get to the hardtack, which he managed to do just as Grandpa shifted to a new topic.

"Now, about this War......" Joshua looked up to see his mother's lips quivering. She pulled Baby George back into her lap, where he contented himself with the hardtack he'd dipped in the gravy, now dripping from his elbow.

Was Ma laughing or crying? Meeting her eyes and seeing her smile, Joshua decided it was both—something he understood clearly after a night of rapid-fire emotions. Her tears were probably about Andrew, the laughter on account of Baby George's antics—certainly she wasn't laughing at Grandpa, like Joshua was close to doing.

He couldn't hold it any longer. Neither could his siblings. Grandpa surely heard the giggling, but kept right on. Whether he would have gotten to the Amen quicker because of it or prolonged the prayer even more, they'd never know.

"I see the Mullins!" Tom shouted as he tore out to greet his favorite playmates, leaving the back door wide open. Eight-year-old Mary with Betsy, six, eagerly jumped from the back of the wagon and joined hands with Tom as the three danced in a circle.

Joshua sighed. No parents were more patient than Sam

and Olivia Mullins; they would have to be to put up with those shrieking girls. But how on earth was *he* going to stand them every day from here on out? That was the question.

Sam brushed off Lucy's apologies for being behind schedule as the girls settled down to sit alongside their parents in the parlor rockers. Tom squeezed in beside Betsy.

Joshua had never seen his mother eat so fast. Was she that nervous or just eager to get on the road? "Could you help me with some sewing?" she soon asked Olivia. "I need to put the finishing touches on the little smocks I made for Jenny and the baby." Setting her plate near the washbowl, she grabbed the drawstring pouch, and reached for Olivia's hand, not waiting for an answer. They closed the bedroom door behind them, leaving the two men to sit and shrug.

Lucy was a fine seamstress. Like the majority of housewives, she did her work entirely by hand since only the wealthiest could afford a sewing machine. What was puzzling, she'd only had scraps to work with for the last two years and hadn't sewn a single garment unless somebody needing her expertise showed up with all the materials. So why was sewing such a priority all of a sudden?

"Have you got that map finished?" Homer asked.

"Yes," Sam said, pulling a piece of paper from his shirt pocket. "Thanks for your help getting started last night. See what you think. Seems to me the hardest part of the journey will be getting to Westport. Once there, we can ask other travelers what they're doing, though it's doubtful we'll find many from this neck of the woods going up to Iowa."

Ten minutes later, the women emerged to show off the colorful new patches on the front of the smocks.

"Is this a new style?" Grandpa asked.

"What do you mean?" exclaimed Lucy, pretending to be offended. "Don't you think they're cute? I figured, rough as this trip will be on everything, it would be nice to have a double layer of fabric in front."

"Oh, I see. This way, when they get dirty, you just rip the patches off and have some clean spots to wipe their hands on," Grandpa teased. "Good idea, Lucy—saves work and soap, too."

Just seconds later, everyone in the room instantly froze at the sound of horses' hooves. "Heaven help us," Lucy whispered loudly. "We don't need any more unexpected company."

Learn more foods available to the Carters in 1863, including recipes you can make yourself, at: http://**justfollowingorders.takecourage.org**

and

http://www.civilwar.org/education/pdfs/civil-war-curriculum-food.pdf

10

"Anybody I know still around these parts?" somebody shouted. "Or is this old mare and wagon now owned by other than Sam Mullins?"

"It's Rev. Miller!" Joshua exclaimed as everyone sprang toward the door.

"Lucy's fresh out of mashed potatoes," Grandpa declared, scampering off the porch and out to help Mrs. Miller down from the wagon. "Maybe we'll find a cup of cold water, though." It was a standard joke of his every time the minister came to visit. The whole family knew how the man loved mashed potatoes.

"A cup of cold water is about all we need, Homer," the pastor assured him. "Sadie and I were just hoping you'd still be here."

Unlike the vast majority of ministers in those days, Rev. Miller refused to ignore the part of the United States Constitution that forbids ministers to use their pulpits for political speeches. However, in private he made it clear that he would never support the Confederacy.

"United We Stand, Divided We Fall," Joshua remembered hearing him say on several occasions from the pulpit. This was the state slogan of Kentucky, from where the minister had come. He thought it was a good one for the entire nation.

"I will continue reminding everyone who will listen: the problems of this nation were created by men, not God," Joshua remembered hearing him saying, back when he was only ten.

His parents talked about this all the way home. "Problem is, people don't want to hear about love and peace if the message suggests a change of hearts on *both* sides," Pa said.

None of the Carters had seen Rev. Miller since they'd left him digging graves at Lone Jack. Shortly afterward, Confederate sympathizers in his congregation were threatening his life, slinging guns and bottles of whiskey at the same time. Like Cyrus, he'd gone into hiding, often sleeping between rows of tall corn.

So he and Mrs. Miller were thrilled when the invitation came for them to move to Kansas City, near the military station, where Unionist views were much more valued. Word was that the Union had since confiscated the church in Pleasant Hill for military use, same as they'd done with many church buildings throughout Missouri.

Of course, the Millers had never even seen Baby George, the minister's namesake. Eagerly Sadie Miller took the baby in her arms, admiring his head of curly brown hair. Next she began taking note of how each of the other children had grown.

How Joshua hated such foolish remarks! As if it was odd for a boy to grow at all. So he was relieved when she offered him just a handshake and simple hello.

Oddly, Rev. Miller seemed not to notice anyone after greeting Grandpa. He kept looking out toward the river. "Where's Cyrus?" He sounded worried. A hush fell over everyone.

"We need to talk," Lucy said softly. She called to Billy who was now chasing Betsy and Mary around the barn. "Come load these things in the cart," she told him, pointing to a conglomeration of odd tools, cooking pots, and dishes she'd managed to round up during the early morning rush. Nearby, a washboard and several bars of homemade soap were stacked. Close to the steps were blankets, a knapsack full of small food items, a jug of drinking water, and a big box of candles next to several tin candle holders she'd bought from Uncle John. Off to the side lay a stack of school books. "When you get finished, take all the younger children to the barn," she added.

She turned to Joshua. "You can come inside soon as you take the Miller's horses out to the watering trough." If she noticed her boys exchanging looks, she didn't let on. Billy looked overwhelmed. Joshua couldn't hide his amusement. It was high time Ma began shifting some of the load to his younger brother.

Putting her arm around Mrs. Miller, Lucy led her guests into the house to break the sad news.

"Cyrus is missing," she said, once they were seated. "He went to help Charlotte and her family after the massacre in Lawrence. A messenger came ten days ago to say Cyrus arrived there and should be home in a few days, but he's still not returned."

"Oh, Lord, help us! What happened?" cried Rev. Miller. Both he and his wife immediately began weeping. "I'm the one who sent that message. I knew he was in Lawrence," he sobbed. "In fact, I saw him there. He should have been home last week."

"You were there, too?" Lucy's question sounded more like an

exclamation. She had to wait several minutes for a response. These friends, most accustomed to comforting others, now needed time to absorb the shock.

The minister cleared his throat several times before he was able to speak. "Yes, my father and older brother, Josiah, live in Lawrence. Not knowing if they were dead or alive, I hired a team of horses and went over the same evening as the raid. Fortunately, they were fine.

I was there when Cyrus arrived, in fact…. saw him down the street from Josiah's place, loading supplies into his wagon. I remember how upset he was about what happened to John Speer and his family. Poor man lost two of his three sons and had his newspaper business destroyed, too. Of course, throwing those presses into the river doesn't arrest free thought any more than it arrests the current of the river. The presses can be replaced, unlike those precious sons."

"Oh, please, tell us more about it all," pled Homer.

The minister sighed deeply. "Like Lone Jack, it was such a terrible tragedy," he moaned. "Yet none of these invaders were true soldiers. Soldiers are supposed to go after other soldiers. Quantrill went after innocent, unarmed, private citizens. At least a dozen women lost *both* a son and husband. Their lives will never be the same, even if the city becomes stronger than ever, which I expect it will. Quantrill claims he's taught his men to not hurt women and children. Obviously, that's untrue. Many of these kids saw their own fathers shot before their eyes. Or their bodies burned by those rascals. Can you imagine anything more hurtful?

"Cyrus and I worked together with many others. Some dug graves. Others went house to house caring for the wounded. All the while, we comforted survivors waiting for the mass funeral.

"Homer, your daughter and son-in-law are reasonably well,"

he assured his friend. "Despite Spencer's leg wound, when I left there, the doc thought he'd be back walking again in a few weeks. Spencer managed to appear dead soon after he was shot, much to the dismay of his screaming wife and children. Good thing he did, though. Otherwise, they probably would have shot him again."

"We came here this morning, assuming Cyrus would be helping to pack the wagon," said Mrs. Miller. "I'm so sorry he's not."

"I'd love to be packing a wagon!" Lucy exclaimed. "We're putting everything we can in the little cart, hoping our balky old mule will get us to Iowa."

"How awful!" cried Mrs. Miller.

"Awful, indeed!" her husband agreed. After drying his eyes, he pulled an envelope from his shirt pocket. "Lucy, I received a letter from Cyrus yesterday … might shed some light on his disappearance."

Joshua, standing in the doorway, rushed forward, not wanting to miss a single clue.

"Cyrus first gives an eloquent description of the atrocities in Lawrence, telling how he was inspired from just being around the survivors. The story demonstrates both the best and worst of humanity. He also gives details of his plans to come home. According to the letter, two businessmen from Lawrence were set to travel as far as Westport with him last Monday," the minister explained. "He was to come on home that same day."

"Sounds like we need Charlotte to tell us if the two companions got back to Lawrence safely," said Sam.

Rev. Miller nodded. "I'm personally going to do everything to investigate, including going to see General Ewing himself," he said. "I'm warning you, it may not be easy, though. That man took issue with one of my sermons recently. Then, last week I pled with him not to go through with Order No. 11. Obviously, he didn't listen."

Taking paper and pencil from his shirt pocket, the visitor scribbled a note, handing it to Lucy. "Soon as you get settled, write me at this address. I'll keep you informed of what I learn." He carefully placed the letter back in the envelope. "This is yours to keep," he said.

Eagerly, she reached out and was soon giving her full attention to her husband's words, though Joshua seemed not to notice.

"I know right where to put the letter," he said, scooping the tin box off the counter and glancing at the minister before thrusting the treasure box into his hands. "Look what I dug up this morning!"

Removing the lid, the pastor's eyes immediately fell on Cyrus' words of August 17. "All we can do now is live for peace," he read aloud before looking at the boy, standing and awaiting his reaction. "I've known about your pa's box for some time," he continued. "It's what kept his active mind occupied while hiding. He hid everything he wrote for fear his words would be used against him. Be careful who sees the contents, Joshua. Once you get to a safer place, though, pull it out and read it often." He thumbed through, selected another page, and handed it up to his young friend.

Joshua read the words very slowly. "It says, 'Slavery is wrong; and wrong always leads to trouble. There is absolutely no reason that reasonable people should allow it to continue. Yet it needs to stop by peaceful, moral means.'" He looked at Rev. Miller. "There's no date on this one," he said. "When do you think it was written?"

"Well, it *could* have been written by someone besides your pa. Even back in 1776, considering how men like Thomas

Jefferson and George Washington were truly convinced slavery was wrong. Yet they weren't ready to act on their convictions, felt a compromise was necessary to keep the Union together. They weren't willing to make the immense personal sacrifice of their own way of life and livelihood either."

"Yes, I've known all about that since I was Billy's age," Joshua politely returned. "But this is Pa's handwriting."

The minister nodded in agreement. "I'd say he wrote that in the fall of 1860," he replied, leaning around to glance at the back side of the paper still in Joshua's hands. "Yes, says right here: 'November 4, 1860, from George Miller's sermon.'" He winked at Joshua and grinned.

"Seriously, though, you better question anything you see with my name on it," he said. "Sometimes I say things that don't make a lot of sense, especially to those who wish to see me silenced forever. I hate to admit it, but some things I say don't make much sense to me either," he mused.

Joshua's whole body shook with laughter, though he never made a sound.

"Before we put this letter away, I want to read something aloud myself, Joshua. It's your father's last paragraph." It was Lucy speaking. All eyes turned to her smiling face.

"Charlotte has me convinced, Lucy is right," she read." We need to be somewhere safer. When I get back, I want to talk to her about going to Iowa with Sam and Olivia." She handed the folded letter back to Joshua.

"Just what we're doing," she said before turning to Sadie Miller. "Thanks to you, I can head north without a single doubt."

11

"Can we? Can we?" Tom and the three girls danced around, jumping up and down, all the while begging Sam to let them ride in the wagon together.

"Okay, you can start out in the wagon," he told them, "but if we see the horses are getting slowed down with the extra weight, some of you will need to ride in the cart."

The ear-splitting squeals went on unceasingly until they got to the main road, but Baby George squealed loudest of all.

Meanwhile Billy and Joshua trudged along in silence. The hot sun overhead was bad enough, but their bare, burning feet on the road was even worse.

Until now, they hadn't minded bare feet. They'd hardly been out of the house long enough to notice. Ma promised they'd be looking for new shoes right away in Kansas City.

After ten minutes on the road, the frolic in the wagon turned to fighting. A quick stop and six-year-old Tom was promptly removed. "You can walk with the rest of us or take a nap in the cart," Lucy told him when he complained.

Tom chose the cart, of course; but he wasn't about to take a nap. The peace didn't last long at all. Boredom was never a problem for that child because he loved to sing. He could sing louder than he could yell, always shrill and off key.

"Flies in the buttermilk, shoo, shoo, shoo," he confidently crooned. It didn't seem to bother Tom when nobody joined in on the familiar words of "Skip to My Lou." In fact, after the "cats in the cream jar," he went right on to "cows in the cornfield," and started over....then over....and over again.

Joshua knew better than to complain. All he could do was hope Ma would soon tire of the noise, but she'd likely think it was cute. Tom never seemed to get scolded like the older boys.

Just Following Orders

The racket went on almost an hour until ... With streams of sweat rolling down his back and eyes half closed, the young mule driver trudged on--bored, hungry, thirsty, and downright exhausted. Surely, they'd be stopping soon.

"Mr. Mullins, how much longer before we get to the first stop near Hickman Mills?" he asked when somehow he'd managed to sprint to the front of the wagon.

"Over two miles to go," Mullins replied. "But there's no plan to stop *there* ... Remember? Our first rest will be at the next stream, about three miles north of town .... Get you a swig of water from the jug on the other side of the wagon while you study the map." He leaned over, pulled a wrinkled piece of paper from his back pocket, and quickly thrust it into the boy's hand. "I think I got the stream drawn pretty close to where it is."

Back in step, Joshua decided to think of something cool and pleasant ... which led to thoughts of the treasure box in the cool soil ... which got him thinking about breakfast....which led to the letter from Pa and Rev. Miller's funny remarks about his own sermon ... which finally took him to a few days after Pa last returned from Westport.

12

To celebrate, they'd had quite a feast. It included a wild turkey, shot by Grandpa with his air rifle. Ma stuffed it with cornbread and walnuts, sent by Mrs. Owsley as Joshua stood beside her whipping cream with a fork for the pumpkin pies.

However, what happened after supper was almost as much fun as the meal.

Like most boys, he relished any opportunity he got to listen in on conversations his parents thought they were having in secret. Yet few boys ever have the advantage of a front-row seat as he'd enjoyed for years from his overhead spot in the loft. That particular night, with conversation especially interesting, he crawled to the very edge of the loft, his soft quilt in tow, determined not to miss a thing on the "stage" below.

"So were you well fed and cared for at the Wornall's?" asked Ma.

"Oh, was I!" Pa exclaimed. "What a hospitable family--rich, but not an ounce of stinginess in them. The way they share what they have, it's no wonder people flock to visit them from all over the country. Interesting what John Wornall gives as the reason for his hospitality. He says God requires it."

Straightening his back, Cyrus stood and took on an air of dignity like he used to do in the classroom whenever he mimicked a man of high rank. "'I try to take seriously the importance of entertaining strangers,' says he. 'That's why we always have our guest rooms ready. Everyone's welcome. That's always been my policy."

"Quite dangerous for these days," Ma declared.

Pa shrugged. "He's living what he believes."

"I can see why the two of you got along so well."

"You know me, Lucy." Pa gazed into her eyes, grinning. "I do have a tendency to take risks," he admitted. "Unfortunately, the ones I take don't pay off like so many of the financial ones John has taken, though.

"I'm glad Joshua got to meet John two years ago," he continued. "Of course, back then he was too young to understand what an important man he was meeting …. Still is, I suppose, but that boy is learning fast."

"Yes he is," Lucy acknowledged. "But so many things he can't understand about this war. I know many boys his age are off fighting like men, but the idea of him doing that just horrifies me."

"It will never happen, Lucy. Not as long as I'm alive," Cyrus assured her.

"Well, that's what worries me. I don't know how long you *will* be alive if we stay around here, Cyrus. It's more dangerous to be against the war than to fight in it. Hard on the family, too, if you get arrested."

"I know Lucy, but we can't afford to leave now. Anyway, surely people will come to their senses and stop this fighting soon."

"Cyrus Carter, when will you ever learn that what you believe isn't what makes sense to most people?"

Joshua wasn't sure what prompted his mother to quickly cover her mouth. Was she startled by how loud she'd shouted or because of what she said? Either way, she must have been as shocked as Pa.

The eavesdropper identified easily with his mother's sentiments. It often angered him, too, thinking of how his father's risks were hurting the whole family. He'd just never heard Ma express her feelings so clearly about anything.

Just as quickly as she'd escalated, her voice mellowed. "Now, what else besides being a risk-taker do you have in common with Mr. Wornall?" she asked, twisting her mouth to one side.

"Well, he and his wife Eliza are both southerners—not from

53

Tennessee, though," Cyrus replied, ignoring his wife's flirtation. "Like George Miller, they come from Kentucky and hate the war as much as we do. They also have had the awful experience of losing children. Just three years ago, a toddler and a set of newborn twins all died in less than a month's time. You and Eliza would have a lot to talk about. ... I do wish you could meet, Lucy."

Joshua was never sure if his father's sudden shift had more to do with his last comment or what he was about to say. Regardless, Cyrus put his head in his hands and stared at the table. "John Wornall is a man of means and great accomplishment while I'm a poor, unemployed school teacher. Otherwise, I guess we're more alike than different, except....

"After all those weeks in their home, I never was able to decide if John is Confederate or Unionist. We talked often far into the night. Yet the more he said, the more confused I became. I must admit, he seems to understand the complicated issues better than anyone I've ever met, though." He paused.

"Eliza's interesting, too. Her father, the Rev. Thomas Johnson brought slaves with him from Kentucky when he started the Shawnee Indian Mission. And he kept buying young females to help at the school until it closed last year." He sighed, shaking his head in disbelief. "Think of what those Indian children were learning, Lucy."

"How, of all people, could ministers ever justify owning slaves?" she exclaimed.

"It's something I also struggled to understand throughout my entire visit. John isn't a minister, but he's a prominent church leader."

"Presbyterian?"

"No, Baptist, and his father-in-law is Methodist. So he certainly has the inside story. John goes back and forth on the slavery issue himself. He still owns four slaves. As he sees it, our nation is fighting a war between two religions, the southern Christians and the northern Christians. Says it's like they're listening to two different gods. He claims if the beliefs hadn't gotten so twisted around, folks might be sitting down, having civil conversations like he and I did, without attacking one another. It sure got me thinking.

"*Separate* gods, you say? Don't both sides call themselves Christians?"

"Yes, but it seems the Christian God in the North thinks entirely different than the Christian God in the South." They both chuckled.

"The way he explains it, ministers on both sides keep stirring the raging flames. They've promoted much of the killing because each is trying to say that what they believe is condoned by a perfect deity. This leads people to see their enemies as evil and violence as condoned."

At that point, Joshua doubted if any of his siblings were still sleeping. Pa was almost yelling, while his mother reverted to more subdued tones.

"Hm-m-m," she said. "Sort of sounds like folks have made gods into their own image."

"That's a good way of putting it," he remarked. "Next time I see John, I must remember to tell him that, Lucy. Now, there's something else I didn't know. The three largest denominations in the South (Methodists, Baptists and Presbyterians, that is) all seceded, so to speak, from those in the North. They did it *over slavery* as much as seventeen years before any state seceded. What's more, many of the southern ministers stepped right in to help their churches see slavery as a gift from God."

"A gift, you say? I thought it was their job to prick people's conscience. How did things get so turned around?" she asked.

"Well, it seems ministers needed to soothe their *own* conscience," he replied. "Most seminaries are located in the

North, and graduates usually leave as firmly convinced of slavery being wrong as Patrick Henry thought it was. Back in 1773, he called it 'destructive to liberty.'"

"Since the rich plantation owners control most everything in the South, they came up with a scheme to serve them well in antebellum days. First, they offered the ministers nice salaries to lure them down. Next, they gave them gifts—slaves to own and daughters to marry."

"Oh, my!" Lucy cried. "Hard not to be swayed by all that." No wonder they needed to change their minds about slavery. So what words could they find to justify it?"

"Well, it goes something like this." Pa stood and pointed his finger at his wife as if she was his captive congregation. "We know all good things come from God," he said, mockingly. "How do we know? Why, we can see for ourselves! Slavery is a good thing because it brings prosperity. Prosperity is always proof that something is good, so slavery comes from God."

"And if a person steals a bag of gold without getting caught, the gold is a gift from God?" his wife questioned.

"Exactly." He said, raising his fists for emphasis. "So when an abolitionist says to a southerner that slavery is an evil institution, the southerner comes back with, 'How dare you so arrogantly insult our God!'"

"Well, did anyone ask the slaves if it's good?" she quizzed.

"Why, of course not! What would they know?" he said, still using his entertaining antics. "Africans are the 'sons of Ham,' which means they were cursed by ignorance and inferiority long ago in the days of Noah."

"Please tell me that's all."

"Oh, I'm afraid not," Pa replied, now resuming his normal voice.

Lucy sighed. "I don't see how it could get any worse."

"Well, listen to this: 'Great good has come to the slaves, people say, because slavery provided a way to bring these heathen to Christianity.' This means the slaves owe their souls to their masters."

"What about all those who didn't survive the voyage across the ocean? I guess their souls don't count?"

Joshua saw his father smile. "According to these newly enlightened ministers, Christians make *fine* slave masters."

"As any slave can tell you who's ever been beaten by one," Lucy declared, knowingly. "So I suppose they don't talk about what happens if a good slave master dies or incurs a debt and has to sell the slave to a cruel master." She scanned her husband's face. "Does John Wornall really believe all this nonsense himself?"

"No. I don't think he does. He says slavery was a big mistake from the beginning, something that our nation has allowed to go on far too long. Yet much like Washington and Jefferson, he can't bring himself to turn loose of the personal benefits.

"Lucy, I can see how easy it would have been for us to have gotten used to slavery ourselves," he continued. "I'm glad we chose not to go that way, though we could have afforded to at one time."

"I'm glad, as well," Lucy agreed.

"So what about the ministers who preach abolition by force," she asked. "Do they claim to have a special understanding of God, like proslavery men?"

"Oh, yes. The most radical even say there *must* be shedding of blood to make men do the right thing. They speak of how God condones the killing of the slave holders. Of course, this means that they think it fine to violently take the law into their own hands rather than go through due process.

"I want to see the slaves free as much as anyone, but these radical abolitionists have made no preparations on behalf of the slaves. Nobody has." His speech accelerated. "When I told John I believe the newly-freed slaves need to be given sufficient aid to allow them to start a new life, he just smiled and raised his eyebrows like it was a good joke. Naturally, compensating slaves is even less likely to be considered than President Lincoln's proposal of compensated emancipation, which Missouri recently rejected."

"You mean his plan for the government to first buy the slaves from their masters and eventually set them free?" Lucy asked.

"Yes," he answered. "Lincoln was convinced if Missouri should go for it, there'd be hope for the rest of the nation to follow. But Lincoln had to badger our state leaders to even talk about it. Still, they didn't talk long, wouldn't even consider it. Some of the slave owners complained they wouldn't be getting enough money while others said it would cost too much. I say it would be a lot less expensive than carrying on this war for another year."

"And that's not even speaking of the lives lost and families destroyed," Lucy added. "It reminds me of how our boys sometimes try to slug out their differences instead of talking."

Pa glanced at his pocket-watch. "It's already past midnight, Lucy. I should go."

At that moment, Joshua pledged to stay awake every night he possibly could. Nothing was more interesting than these things he wasn't supposed to hear. ... Too young, eh? Ridiculous! After all, he'd even been to a battlefield—something Ma couldn't claim.

He recalled fondly how she'd slid around the corner of the table and snuggled next to Pa. That's when he blew out the candle, leaving Joshua with nothing to do but ponder the meaning of everything he'd seen and heard.

And that's just what he was doing now, almost asleep on

his feet, not noticing that Old Nelly was trotting fast as a bullet toward a pool of murky water, just over a ditch where Tom, now sleeping soundly atop the cart, was about to land.

13

Suddenly all the contents of the cart lay strewn from the edge of the road all the way to where Old Nelly stood quenching her thirst.

"Joshua Carter!" his mother shouted. "We'll never get to Iowa at this rate."

"What happened?" Tom, covered with flour, called from the ditch. He ran to the wagon in spite of his humiliation as the three girls rolled in side-splitting laughter.

Joshua saw nothing to laugh about. What a disaster! Already, he'd let his mother down, and it wasn't even close to noon. Certainly, Old Nelly was no laughing matter. Neither was his habit of falling asleep in the daytime, nor his frequent daydreaming, which his parents always teased him about. It was a habit he'd started the year Andrew began coming over to fish. Both of them knew how to dream—whether alone or together.

"I wonder what it would be like to live in New York City," Andrew said as he and Joshua dangled poles over the water. *"Pa says they don't even have trees for blocks and blocks in the middle of that town. He says the black smoke from the factories makes the sky look grey instead of pretty blue like we see here in Missouri."*

Joshua couldn't imagine. "Have you seen pictures?" he asked Andrew.

"No, but my pa knows all about it. Says those folks are strange up there. I don't care about ever leaving Missouri, do you?"

"Oh! NO! Not me," Joshua agreed. "I like it right here beside the Little Blue River."

Jarred back to the present, he heard his mother yell: "Joshua! Billy! Quickly! Gather things up. We don't want to be here any longer than necessary." She put Baby George on the ground beside her, for once seeming not to care that he was wailing, but offered no explanation for her anxiety.

Joshua was puzzled. He saw nothing as alarming as what he'd witnessed before breakfast that morning.

Somehow, Grandpa seemed to understand. "Lucy, don't worry. We'll just follow the plan we talked about last night," he called over his shoulder while climbing onto the wagon seat beside Mrs. Mullins. Grabbing the reins, he soon had the horses trotting faster than they'd run all day. Sam Mullins was nowhere in sight!

Ma hissed. "Do not ask questions. I'll explain when we catch up with them at supper."

"What's this?" Billy's laugh broke the tension. "Ma, you told Joshua and I not to put anything unnecessary in this cart. Just look what I found."

It was the sign from above Grandpa's bed. Baby George, apparently calmed by the laughter of the other three, was squealing for joy again.

"I'm sure *Grandpa* would say this sign is absolutely necessary," their mother said. "He would make a silly joke about it—maybe something like how it could be his tombstone in case he bites the dust before we get to Iowa."

Her remark fell flat. Too late, she realized how morbid her intended joke had sounded. Billy tossed the sign into the cart, slinging a small, dingy knapsack right behind it.

Quickly, Lucy rushed over. She rearranged several items,

carefully tucking the knapsack under everything else. "What I have in that knapsack is more important than anything in the cart," she said emphatically. Joshua shook his head in disbelief.

"What could possibly be so important about a sack of raggedy, old clothes?" he asked. He got no answer.

With the cart finally reloaded, he took his position to the left of Old Nelly. Ma fell into line on her right, with instructions for Billy to stay close to his brother in case the mule got any more wild ideas. She was taking no chances.

All Joshua could think about was the stream ahead. He longed for cool, fresh water.

They were soon delayed again, though it wasn't Old Nelly's fault this time. Nor was it Joshua's.

A young woman, about sixteen, sat next to a toddler. "Just resting," she told Lucy who stopped to inquire. On her lap, lay two tiny babies. Over her shoulder, a knapsack no larger than the one his mother just placed in the cart.

Her name was Nora. She had no definite plans. Though from Hickman Mills, she'd been turned away from the military station for having kin among bushwhackers. Joshua didn't need to think twice about what to do next.

"Ma'am, we've got some soft blankets in the cart," he said. Reaching down, he gently took one of the babies and helped her to her feet while Lucy reached for the toddler.

"His name's Jeremiah," stated Nora.

"Well, Jeremiah," Lucy said to the boy. "You and Baby George may want to take a nap while Old Nelly clops on. The child quickly grabbed onto the chunk of hardtack he was handed and gnawed it as if he'd not eaten all day.

Soon the women were chatting more like a mother and daughter, with the twins looking over their shoulders. Now having four escorts, Old Nelly *had* no choice but to cooperate.

By the time they found the stream, Joshua had almost

forgotten his own problems. For weeks, he and his family had been thinking only of their own survival. Now, he realized, there were others much worse off. What did Nora plan for her children to eat? Were the things in the knapsack all she owned or simply all she could carry? Had her house been among those already burned? She offered few clues. Respectfully, Ma asked no questions.

"Seems we should have come to that stream already," Joshua kept saying. "Maybe Mr. Mullins forgot just where it was." Oddly, his mother didn't complain at all. She moved along, chatting with Nora, as if taking a Sunday afternoon stroll. Fortunately, she'd grabbed a spare jug of water just before the rest of the party sped off. Though almost boiling now, at least it kept them from dying of thirst.

It was sunset when they finally spotted the wagon. Mr. Mullins had parked in a cluster of trees, away from the road, for his own protection, as well as the horses. Nothing was more prized by the guerrillas than a good horse. They brought premium prices.

Famished, everyone got to work gathering firewood. Soon Mrs. Mullins had a kettle filled with fresh, boiled corn and a skillet of hot gravy to soften the hardtack.

After supper, Nora took her little family and started walking again. She hoped to find a house where she could rest or maybe someone else traveling who would help her get on to Westport. There she had cousins who might have a room, she said.

Joshua, more exhausted than he could ever recall being, made a bed under the wagon. He felt so comfortable here in the woods—strangely, more comfortable than back home in the loft. Not only was the ground a little softer than the floor back home. Somehow, sleeping outdoors made him feel closer to his father.

Best of all, he was less anxious since Grandpa and Billy agreed to sit by the road until 2:00 a.m. with the dogs next to the cart. Then, with their shift over, Lucy and Joshua would watch until breakfast. Each pair would pretend to be alone, resting for a few hours, with just an old mule and half-empty cart to get them where they were going. That way, maybe any unwelcome visitors wouldn't suspect there was a hidden wagon near the water.

Joshua was too tired to care, but he wondered to himself why Mr. Mullins had hardly left the wagon and was apparently planning to sleep all night. Adults! Sometimes they didn't make a bit of sense.

About midnight, he woke just in time to catch the sound of his mother and grandfather's muffled conversation from a few feet away. "So have they been gone long?" his mother asked.

"Maybe thirty minutes," Grandpa replied. "Billy and I sat quiet as two church mice until we saw them turn back south, 'round the last bend in the road."

"So what did they want?" It was Mr. Mullin's voice now.

"Just money," Homer replied. From what Joshua could see in the faint moonlight, his grandpa seemed to be studying his mother's face for a reaction. "I'm afraid they got all we had. I tried, Lucy, but I couldn't stop them. They held a knife to my throat."

Instantly, Joshua sprang to his feet while his mother dashed to the cart. Reaching in, she pulled up the knapsack, felt inside, and hugged it to her, smiling. "So what did they take?" she asked Grandpa.

"At first, only the fifty cents I had in my pocket," he replied. "I told them I was totally broke. They didn't believe me. Finally, I was so scared I handed them the tin and told them the truth— that was all the money we owned, Lucy."

He looked devastated until he noticed his daughter-in-law covering her mouth and giggling like a school girl. "You only gave them three dollars, Homer," she whispered. "Three dollars is all I left in that old tin."

"Three dollars?" he asked, incredulously.

"Yes. Only three dollars," she replied, with a chuckle. "My plan worked!" She glanced at her two sons, then back: "I hid the rest, Homer, hid it well." She had a glint in her eyes that Joshua hadn't seen for months! "Considering how folks expect men to always know where the money is," she continued, "I figured it was better to keep all of the men-folk guessing for a while."

"So that's what your fancy sewing was all about this morning!" Grandpa exclaimed, forgetting to whisper. He winked at Joshua. "Your ma is one smart lady," he declared. Billy and his grandpa turned toward the wagon.

Lucy beamed with pride as she and Joshua prepared to sit through the rest of the night. "So what's on *your* mind, young man?" she asked.

"Questions," he replied. "*Plenty* of questions."

14

Joshua lifted the keg of cornmeal to the ground. With the moonlight too faint for him to see the bottom of the cart, he had to feel around. In their haste to find the money, the thieves had tossed everything to and fro. His heart pounded frantically as his imagination ran wild. If they'd found the treasure box, had they taken it all? Come daylight, would he discover an empty tin tossed in the grass? Once they started reading those secret messages, what might they do? Come back and ask lots of questions and take him off to parts unknown? Maybe they'd keep searching and find the wagon with Mr. Mullins in it. If so, how would they ever get to Iowa without their guide?

To him, the tin box had grown more valuable with each and every step yesterday. To keep his mind occupied, he'd spent hours formulating plans for how to use it, maybe adding more to the collection. In his best daydream, he and his father were together again, examining the contents with Pa explaining why he'd chosen to save each piece.

Suddenly he spotted a glimmer of something shiny. Stretching every muscle, he stood tiptoe, shifting his weight until his right hand felt the cool metal. Yes! He only needed to get his left hand around it and find a way to set his feet back on the ground. Instead he found himself sinking slowly, further and further into the cart, inch by inch, until he abruptly fell into a heap. No matter. He had it. More importantly, judging from the weight, there was a good chance the contents had gone undisturbed.

"Oh-oh!" he moaned, rubbing his aching shoulder. He looked up to see his mother peering down at him.

"Is it all there?" she asked—in fact, that was all she asked. Here he was all banged up and she only cared about the contents of this tin that she'd hardly seemed to notice back at the house. He relinquished it to her outstretched hand and heaved himself over the side and down to the ground, falling into a heap, groaning still.

Quickly, he opened the tin and counted the hand-written pages—sixteen in all, besides all the clippings.

"Every page," he said softly. Carefully, he let the tin drop back into the corner nearest him and put the keg of corn meal back on top. "I'm glad those bandits didn't find it," he said.

"I suppose it was the first thing you located when the cart was upset?"

"Oh, yes. And the first thing I put back in," he assured her. "Just like you taking care of the old knapsack. Ma, this is the most important thing I own now."

"I understand, but it may end up being a serious problem

for us. I'm worried, Joshua. Not sure we should run the risk of keeping that tin after what just happened," she declared.

"Oh! Ma, please!" he begged. "I can't wait to see what was so important to Pa that he'd bury these things in the same hole with his life savings."

"We'll just hope they stay hidden, then. Along with all the other secrets boys your age hide," she teased.

"Me? What about *you*? So did you run a needle and thread through the money yesterday while you were sewing, or what?"

"Some secrets I'll keep a little longer," she said, laughing.

"I hope not the one about why the wagonload of travelers left us beside the road yesterday without any explanation. I'm dying to know."

"Without any explanation to *you*," Ma corrected. "I understood perfectly."

"What did Grandpa mean about the plan you'd made? Was leaving us behind a part of the plan?" he asked.

"Of course, it wasn't!" she replied. "The original plan was for Mr. Mullins to get into the big, wooden box in the wagon. Grandpa was to take the reins at the same time. That was all about to happen when Old Nelly went off the road." She stopped and sighed deeply. "It's complicated."

"Well, I don't have anything else to do but listen for a few hours," he said, with a hint of sarcasm.

"Then, I'll try to explain." She scanned the sky for the Big Dipper, as if the stars might help her find the right words. "It's about the oath," she offered.

"The *Loyalty* Oath?" he asked. His mother nodded as he rushed on. "Isn't not having one the reason you think Pa is missing? So is Mr. Mullins going to be in the same trouble if he doesn't have one? Or does he have one? And what about Grandpa? Or you? Are just *men* required to carry them?"

"Slow down and I'll try to answer your inquisition, Josh."

Both chuckled. "In Missouri, at least one adult in every family must take the Loyalty Oath," she explained. "As you know, it's especially dangerous to travel without it.

Your father objected to it for several reasons. He thinks it's both unconstitutional and useless because people can pledge to do something, just to stay out of trouble, then turn around and break their pledge. So he never signed it. Yet he's wanted for ignoring the Enrollment Act."

"The Enrollment Act?" Joshua asked.

"That's the new one this year," his mother explained, "calling all men under forty-five to register for military service. Some call it 'the draft.' States who do not have enough volunteers to meet their quota can call men from the registry to fight for the Union.

"Didn't they have something like that last year?" Joshua asked.

"That's another registry—the one for the state militia to help keep the peace in Missouri."

"Loyalty Oath, Militia, Enrollment Act? Ma, I'm getting really confused. So do they have all of this in Kansas, too?"

"No, Kansas doesn't need it all. Union's got plenty of volunteers, and most people there wouldn't think of harboring bushwhackers either," Lucy reminded him. "Plus, they've got a lot of freedmen from Missouri to help fill their quota.

"Well, the Confederates can't say *they* will defend the Union, especially with so many ready to take up arms against the Union. So how come they don't get in trouble?"

"Oh, they can say whatever they want—just like any of us can. People sign the Oath one day and have loyalty papers in their pockets, then invite bush-whackers for dinner the next. As long as they don't get caught, it doesn't matter to most. That's why Mr. Mullins says it's meaningless. And I agree, though Grandpa and I both signed it."

"You did?" Joshua exclaimed. "When?"

"About ten days ago.....Remember when we borrowed Mr. Mullin's wagon and went to Hickman Mills, leaving you to take care of the little ones?"

Joshua nodded slowly. "I *thought* it strange, you went so far for a few vegetables."

"I was very worried about taking you children on the road without us having protection papers."

"Protection papers? I'm confused again." Joshua sounded exasperated.

"Well, this is easier to explain. Protection papers are what a person gets *after* signing the Oath. Any more questions?" Ma asked.

"Yes. Did Mr. Mullins hide in the box because he has no protection papers on account of not signing the Loyalty Oath?"

"That's correct. Are you sure you want me to go on, 'cause it's about to get more complicated."

"Continue." He nodded.

"Listen carefully, then.... Mr. Mullins was raised Quaker. To him, it's not proper to take *any* oath. For Quakers, it's against their religion. Yet that's not always respected. So he fears to even ask if he could get off."

"Huh? What's the problem with taking an oath? If it's wrong, then why don't Presbyterians refuse to take oaths?" he asked.

Once more, Ma sighed. "Could you save that question for another day? It's also complicated, and I'm sure the Mullins can answer much better than I. While you are at it, you can ask him why Quakers don't believe in bearing arms, too—though that's not an issue for Mr. Mullins 'cause he's over 45, the age when the Enrollment Act no longer applies."

"OK. So yesterday, Grandpa took the reins 'cause he *does* have protection papers?"

Ma nodded.

Pointing his index finger toward his mother, Joshua gestured in much the same manner that his father would in the classroom when he had several important points to make. "So he could leave us behind like he did yesterday because you have them, too. But Mrs. Mullins, the men figured, would be assumed to be Grandpa's wife; and Mr. Mullins was hiding in the box—just in case they got stopped."

Ma nodded again. "Yes, and I was counting on the children staying quiet," she said, "like I've told all of you to do anytime a stranger comes around."

"We were lucky it all worked. Yet, when the bushwhackers stopped a few minutes ago, they could have first pretended to be jayhawkers, asked for Grandpa's protection papers, and shot him for having them?"

"I think you have it all figured out, Joshua. Fortunately, the wagon wasn't stopped yesterday, and Grandpa and Billy got through tonight's little robbery better than most. Now, if we can make it past the Missouri River, we'll likely be a lot safer. Definitely so, once we get to Iowa." In the dark, he clearly heard the smile in his mother's voice.

"Just think, Joshua--you'll soon be back in school, meeting new friends and seeing them regularly without worrying about guerrillas every day."

"And you can go to town more often, Ma. You can bring home books and newspapers, too, just like Pa used to. We can start planting crops again."

"Hold on, young man. This will all take time. First we must find a house and some land. Starting over will be hard, especially with your pa gone."

"Ma, do you think we'll find him?" Joshua's voice clearly reflected concern now.

"I sure hope so, Joshua—the sooner, the better."

"The way I see it, Pa's a rebel, too. Just not at all like the

Confederates," Joshua said, for once making a statement rather than posing a question.

"I suppose that's one way of looking at it. Your father is one of few men in the country who would dare rebel against this war by avoiding the draft." She paused. Joshua picked up right where she left off.

"The War of the Rebellion," he mused. "I know southerners don't use that name. What do they call it, Ma?"

"The War for Independence," his mother replied.

"Well, it seems to me both names fit well, depending on how you look at it," he concluded. "The slaves are rebelling against slavery and fighting for their independence at the same time. Of course, I know the rebels see themselves as the real victims. Guess there's a lot of ways to rebel—being a rebel can be a good way to make change when change is needed. Or it can just create pain and chaos for everyone when a needed change is resisted."

Lucy was nodding off. But when he suddenly stopped talking, she jolted upright. Wrapping her arms around him, she squeezed him tighter than she had in a long time.

"Unless you have more questions, I'd like to rest a while before making a big batch of johnnycakes," she said.

Thinking of johnnycakes made him famished. So he sat in silence, soon dropping to the ground, fast asleep.

15

Sam Mullins had the horses hitched and was rearing to roll before daybreak, but Joshua couldn't pick himself up off the ground—until Baby George leaped into the center of his belly.

With eyes wide open, he bounded to a sitting position just in time for Jenny to hand him a tall plate of johnnycakes.

"You're getting pampered this morning," Mrs. Mullins said, handing him a cup of her special "coffee." Real coffee had been in short supply for two years. Joshua liked the substitute, though, which pleased her immensely since neither Sam nor anyone else she knew could stop pining for the real thing long enough to appreciate the work. About once a week, she'd peel half a dozen sweet potatoes, cook the inside for supper, and roast the peels. When they were almost burned, she ground them down to the size of coffee grounds. Joshua often helped her, then, stayed around to enjoy a fresh-brewed pot.

"Now let's see what we can do with those feet," she said. She reached for the can of lard beside her and began gently massaging it into the cracks and crusty scabs he'd failed to notice yesterday. "Guess you got a case of tenderfoot from having to stay close to the house so long. Nature will take care of that. A few more days on the road and you'll have calluses thick as horses' hooves."

"Can't somebody get that boy moving?" Grandpa called from near the wagon. "I've already got the cows milked and given Old Nelly her first pep talk of the day."

"I know, Grandpa," Joshua agreed. "Soon as Mrs. Mullins gets finished, I'll get a little cool water from the stream and be ready."

"Stream, you say? What stream?" asked Mr. Mullins, who was now standing by Grandpa.

Mr. Mullins looked perturbed, Joshua just puzzled. "Isn't this the place you planned for us to spend the night?" he asked.

"It didn't work out that way, Joshua," came the reply. The streams we passed were both dried up, trees now being the only evidence they ever existed. So we had to keep pushing on, looking for water yesterday, and didn't find any 'til we got to

71

the Blue River."

"The Blue River? You're joking," said Joshua.

The man shook his head in extra-slow motion. "Never been more serious. We made fourteen miles out of desperation."

Joshua mischievously squinted his left eye, twisting his head in the same direction, trying to look really annoyed. The smirk was a dead giveaway. "Mr. Mullins, do you mean to tell me we're more than halfway to Kansas City already?" he asked.

"Yep. We covered lo-o-ots of ground yesterday," the neighbor confirmed.

Joshua's eyes were both tiny slits now. "So this explains why I'm so tired this morning. I had to walk all fourteen miles while *you* rode in a box."

Mr. Mullins had a comeback. "It also explains why every bone in my body is aching. Today, if I decide to get back in that box, I want two more quilts for padding."

"Grandpa, did we take a wrong turn?" Tom asked. He looked worried. "Why are we back at the Little Blue?"

Joshua could explain that much. "Tom, the Blue River and the Little Blue are two different rivers entirely."

Grandpa knelt down and touched the six-year-old on the shoulder. "This Blue River is wider and a lot closer to Kansas City than the Little Blue, but it's not very blue today nor is it very wide. In fact, I had to wade out to the middle last night to find water fit to drink." He raised his glass. "After letting it sit all night for the sediment to go to the bottom, it looks pretty clear doesn't it? Tastes mighty good, too."

"Since I've never been up this way, I don't know how wide the river normally is. Certainly, with the drought this year, it's down more than usual," said Sam.

"Huh?" Joshua looked at him in disbelief. "If you never were up this way, how did you know where to put the streams on the map in the first place?"

Both men howled. "Your grandpa helped me put that map together. I haven't been this far north since Mrs. Mullins and I came down the *east* side of Jackson County back in 1852. But you and your grandpa were when your pa took you with him to go to Lawrence a while back."

"T'was late fall....of 1860.....just months before the Rebellion," Grandpa spoke slowly like he always did when he had a long, long story to tell. "You remember, don't you, Joshua?"

"Oh, yes! What fun it was seeing Aunt Charlotte and her family over in Lawrence! What I remember most about the big city were all the lights at night, coming from houses so close together. It was a glorious sight."

"Do you remember going to the restaurant in Kansas City, where you got the big steak?" asked Grandpa.

"I remember how you had to help me eat it," Joshua answered, with a nod. "And that's where Pa met Mr. Wornall for the first time. I remember he came to our table, wearing that big top hat, and asked Pa what he was reading."

"Oh, yes. Cyrus was holding the first copy he'd ever owned of *Harper's Weekly*. Couldn't put it down for weeks afterwards," Grandpa recalled. His eyes narrowed, as if this might help him bring back every detail.

Joshua turned to Mr. Mullins, continuing where his grandfather had left off. "Pa showed Mr. Wornall Charles Dicken's story, called 'Great Expectations.' The magazine had just started printing the book, one chapter at a time. That was news to Mr. Wornall, but he was most interested. So he joined us at the table while Pa told him all about this boy named Pip, an orphan in England, who'd lost everything. We all wondered if Pip would survive."

"I remember that story, too," Lucy said. "Cyrus never did find it all in print himself. He sure was excited, though, when Mr. Wornall discovered the last chapters in later issues of the magazine. Cyrus got to read it while in Westport."

"Oh, yes. He came home and told us how Pip had found the true meaning of friendship and love in spite of all his losses," Joshua concluded.

"Of course, back then, your pa had no way of knowing what a fine friend he'd found, nor how many hours he and Mr. Wornall would spend discussing important concerns over the next few years," Grandpa added.

"We're almost to Westport with only ten miles to cover before we're out of Jackson County," Sam stated, "but if we keep standing around here talking, we'll never make it to the Missouri River tomorrow by noon as our plan calls for."

"Don't count your chickens before they hatch, Sam Mullins," Grandpa warned. "The way your plans have been working out so far, I think we should just wait and see what happens next."

To **learn more** about "Great Expectations" and the thirteen other famous novels that Charles Dickens wrote, see:

http://www.dickensfellowship.org/dickens-fiction-writer

16

A half hour later, Tom was the only one making a sound. He sat back on his perch atop the cart, piping out the sixth round of his second favorite tune: "The old gray mare, she ain't what she used to be, ain't what she used to be, ain't what......"

Even above the annoyance, Joshua thought he recognized his name being called from across the road. He must have been mistaken, for how could there be anyone so far from the Little Blue who knew him by name?

"Aren't you Joshua Carter?" he distinctly heard. His tension dissipated soon as he saw the man with the top hat and a smile as bright as the morning's sunshine.

"Mr. Wornall?" Joshua shouted in disbelief. "Is that really you?"

"'Tis me, indeed," his father's dear friend said before reaching out with the firmest handshake Joshua had ever known.

"Oh, Pa! Pa! Stop! Sto-o-p!" Betsy and Mary screamed repeatedly, all the while.

"Joshua's about to get kidnapped!" Betsy kept adding, raising the volume even higher.

Lucy Carter, who had been walking at a fast pace ahead of everyone, immediately darted back to investigate. Seconds later, hearing her son's name spoken, she was both relieved and shocked by the tall, dignified stranger stepping from a gentleman's carriage with sporty, red wheels.

Mr. Wornall glanced toward the wagon, then back at Joshua, his smile brightening further as Joshua's faced turned scarlet due to the scene those silly little girls were making.

"How did you recognize me?" Joshua asked.

"Why, I'd know that crop of auburn hair anywhere." Mr. Wornall declared.

Until now, Joshua had never imagined that his hair color could be an asset. It was just another thing, besides his small stature, to make him feel conspicuous.

His embarrassment faded as the other adults alighted from the wagon to join his mother, already conversing with her husband's good friend.

In fact, Joshua was so focused on all the adults he didn't notice the boy approaching.

Neither did he see the girls cowering in silliness, peering

under the edge of the wagon sheet, until he heard Betsy's exclamation. "Ooh, just look at those big, blue eyes!"

Joshua cast a dirty look at the girls. He felt his face turning warm again. Girls could be so intolerable.

"I'm Frank Wornall," the boy said, approaching Joshua with confidence and polish almost equal to his pa. "Your father is nice. He and I played a lot of checkers last winter."

Nice to meet someone near my own age after months of isolation, thought Joshua, reaching out to shake the boy's hand.

"Maybe you can come to my birthday party," Frank suggested. "I'll be eight in just three weeks."

Joshua worked hard to hide his disappointment and envy. This eight-year-old was a head taller than him.

"Well, hi, Frank," he politely returned. "I'm Joshua, and I'll soon be fourteen. Sorry. I won't make your party. In three weeks, we hope to be in Iowa."

The girls' swooning ceased, but Betsy immediately began complaining of a sore throat. She whined and refused to be consoled, even hours later, when they sat around the big dining table at the Wornall's place, just three miles from where they now stood while Mr. Wornall began formulating plans to make their lives easier from that moment on.

He started by rearranging the passengers in his own vehicle, then each of the other travelers. Jim, the dark-skinned carriage driver, wasn't surprised at his new assignment. Instead of holding the reins, he would walk beside the cows in place of Billy, who would be enjoying the company of Frank inside the carriage. Mrs. Carter and her two youngest children would take the other seat, facing the two boys. Up front, Mr. Wornall would have Joshua squeezed in beside him so he could get caught up with all the past year's news about his wonderful friend Cyrus, he said.

Once again, Tom was given a choice—he could ride in the

carriage with the older boys or join the Mullins in the wagon. He struck a bargain. "I'll take the wagon if I can ride in Mr. Mullin's box," he proposed.

Olivia threw in extra padding and welcomed the singer aboard.

Meanwhile, a lighter-skinned man, who was introduced as "my hired hand, Hans," stepped from inside of the carriage.

"I'll take care of the mule," he told Joshua.

"I'm not sure she'll cooperate," Joshua said, reluctantly.

"Never fear," Grandpa assured him as he alighted from the wagon. "I feel like walking again, and I'm sure Hans and I together can manage her without upsetting the applecart."

"Apples?" cried Tom from his new perch atop the quilts. "I didn't see no apples in that cart."

17

Joshua didn't bother opening his eyes. If he had, he might have known he wasn't dreaming. He hadn't felt so rested since before the Battle of Lone Jack! In fact, he didn't care if he raised his head off the fluffy pillow for the rest of the day.

Yet the voices and fuzzy scenes in his dreams seemed far away, as if his ears were plugged with cotton, his eyes peering through a pair of someone else's spectacles. He could see the large colored woman in a big, white apron. She stood in the center of a porch with four, huge columns, a few feet from a big door of an enormous mansion. "Miz 'Liza, come quick, looks like we got a who-o-ole lot o' comp'ny," she shouted frantically.

A deep, familiar voice, which he promptly recognized as Mr. Wornall's, came next: "This boy's worn out, Hans. Please carry him to the first stranger room and put him to bed while Jim takes care of the animals."

Then, he heard him talking to his mother. "Lucy, from what Joshua just told me, I think you need to let me buy the old mule for a few hundred dollars so you can get to Iowa by the end of next week."

He could feel how his weight shifted in the strong arms that seemed to be transporting him up and up again. There was a sensation of floating on a cloud. It was odd. Any boy over six would probably be embarrassed under such circumstances. Yet he didn't even squirm, and certainly didn't insist on being put down. Instead, he gave in to the heaviness of his exhausted limbs that had him paralyzed.

He must have fallen asleep again—or maybe not. All he knew now was that someone seemed to be scrubbing his dirty feet, then drying them as they dangled off the bed where the rest of his body lay immobile. He sank into the soft bedding again, and again totally lost consciousness.

Hours later, he was fully awake. As soon as his eyes flew open, he knew this was more than a wonderful dream. It was real. Rearing up on his elbows gave him a better vantage point for taking in his surroundings. Thinking of Mr. Wornall offering to give so much for Old Nelly, he laughed aloud. Why, she wasn't worth fifty dollars!

He gazed at the rich woods of the furniture and royal blue curtains with the fancy, matching chair in wonder. Suddenly, he realized that he'd gone from living in a cottage to being homeless and now to sleeping in a mansion--all overnight. And he was starving.

Somebody must have known he'd be starving, though. Right beside him, on a table, sat two big sandwiches, a fresh peach, a thick piece of cake, and the coldest, most delicious, fruit drink he'd ever tasted.

He devoured it all, then went to the open window, and studied the scene below. What was all the cheering about? Obviously, some kind of game he'd never seen before with two teams. Frank Wornall was throwing a small ball, over and over, toward Betsy Mullins. Repeatedly, she swung a big stick, trying to hit the ball, but kept missing. Joshua was quite amused.

Mr. Wornall patiently showed Betsy a better way to hold the stick. "Just keep trying," he told her. And so she did until about the tenth time when the ball went flying over Frank's head, almost hitting Fox, where he lay near the outhouse, oblivious to the intrusion.

Betsy stood in shock. Everyone yelled for her to run to a bare spot in the yard while Frank and Tom chased the ball. By the time she'd made it passed two other bare spots, they told her to "run home." With a look of confusion, she asked where home was. Good question, Joshua thought.

"You have to stay there on third base now," Hans told Betsy. She looked at him questioningly, but bolted off third as soon as he told her to, making it back to where she'd swung the stick. Frank and the older players shouted approval. So that was home, Joshua decided as he joined in the cheering.

Mr. Wornall responded with a smile and a wave. "So you're awake?" he called. "Well, come on out and play baseball."

So *that's* what they called this new game. Rushing outside, he scurried down a flight of stairs, gazing at the enormous house before flying around the nearest corner and stopping again to stare.

Any remaining doubt instantly vanished. The columns in his dream were real. They stood before him, rising up to a balcony outside a beautiful second-floor window. He reached out to

79

touch the one nearest his feet, then threw his arms around it and laughed for sheer joy.

In the next hour, he made four home runs.

To **learn more** about the history of baseball and how it compares to today's game, check this out:

http://www.19cbaseball.com/field.html

18

Joshua worked hard to maintain his dignity as he waited to take his seat at supper. He stared at the fancy, red, glass dishes and string of silverware at each plate. Everything seemed too pretty to touch, and he was afraid of messing it up. Back home, they each got a tin cup and one tin plate with a spoon and fork—nothing else. Their table was bare wood. And they were lucky if they had more than two big bowlfuls of food to share.

No telling how many dresses and shirts Ma could make from the calico tablecloth. What on earth were the handkerchiefs for? They certainly looked too fancy for nose-wiping.

"There aren't enough plates on the table!" exclaimed Billy. His mother stared at him in disbelief. Joshua, mortified beyond words, shot a dirty look across the table before catching the eye of their hostess standing to Billy's left, trying to cover her smirk.

"Please excuse my impulsive son," Lucy said. Her face was scarlet. Her eyes, still pinned to the nearest table leg, slowly moved up the table to where Mr. Wornall stood with his sleeves still rolled up from the afternoon game. "At our house, Billy's in charge of setting the table. Counting plates is one of his specialties."

Mr. Wornall smiled kindly--first at Lucy, then at Billy. "Is it four we're missing?" he asked.

"Yes sir, exactly four," Billy replied. Mr. Wornall nodded.

"Around here, our little ones eat early," he explained. "Jenny and your baby brother are probably already asleep, alongside Ednie and Sallie. Don't worry. Matilda is a fine nanny, takes care of the children like they were her own." He turned his attention to Joshua.

"Considering this is your first time to play baseball, I'd say you boys will soon be star players in Iowa,"

"Do you think they'll know how to play there?" asked Sam Mullins.

"Most certainly," replied their host. "The further north one goes, the more likely a person is to see men and boys playing. The game's a favorite pastime for soldiers in both armies. Once the glorious day comes for all soldiers to get back to normal life, every boy across this nation will be exposed to it. I can foresee teams competing around the country with large crowds coming to watch. Instead of newspapers telling us who won each battle, they'll be reporting the winners of each game."

"Well, at least we might get one good thing from this rebellion," suggested Grandpa. "It seems to me baseball could have somehow caught on without so much heartbreak and ruckus."

"What about girls?" asked Tom, too young to appreciate his grandpa's point. "Will they be on teams like Mary and Betsy were today?"

Frank guffawed. "*Girls* don't play baseball," he said. "Pa just let them play this time so we'd have enough for two teams."

"Well, maybe me and Betsy can start something new," chimed in Mary, who sat beside Frank. Olivia Mullins didn't need to say a word. Her pride was obvious as she gazed into her daughter's eyes.

"As for this awful war, I don't think it will go on much longer after all that transpired at Vicksburg and Gettysburg this summer," suggested Mrs. Wornall a little later. "The South is almost paralyzed now that the Union has complete control of the Mississippi River. "

"I agree, Eliza. What big losses for the Confederacy! It looks like the South might as well surrender." her husband declared. "They have thirty thousand men either captured or missing from the weeks of fighting around Vicksburg alone--not to mention all who were killed!" There was a collective gasp from the other adults. They'd had nothing beyond local rumors for weeks.

"Another recent battle, much closer, and one of great significance is The Battle of Honey Springs," their host continued. "You do know about that one, don't you, Eliza?" he asked.

"No, John. I have no idea what state Honey Springs is in. Tennessee, perhaps?"

"Oh, no. Indian Territory," he informed her.

"Could you tell us more about it, Mr. Wornall?" Joshua asked, thinking back to his conversation with his grandfather recently.

"It happened just days after Vicksburg and Gettysburg. Confederates lost again—this time perhaps because it rained and got their ammunition soaked. Most amazing battle—more than half the soldiers on both sides being either Negro or Indian. Some people might think it odd, but many of the Indians have been fighting for the Confederacy. Some of them even own slaves.

"So what made the battle so significant?" Joshua wanted to know.

"Oh, with that victory the Union was able to go on to Ft. Smith, Arkansas, to gain control there. That about sewed it up for the Union on this side of the Mississippi."

During the discussion about Honey Springs, Aunt Molly and a boy she called Pete were busy clearing the table. If they were even listening, they gave no indication. Mr. Wornall paused to glance around the table.

"Maybe you wonder why I'm not being more discreet in speaking of political matters around my slaves. Well, it doesn't matter what they hear because they aren't slaves anymore." He cast a patronizing smile toward Aunt Molly. "I gave them their freedom a few days after President Lincoln signed the Emancipation Proclamation in January. I didn't have to. Those of us in border states aren't required to—at least not yet. Smart move on Mr. Lincoln's part: he can't afford to lose a one of the border states. No doubt emancipation is something everyone must soon face, like it or not, unless the Confederacy suddenly manages to turn things around. What I did was a gesture of gratitude to my servants for all their years of service, though."

Joshua had almost given up trying to understand such strange and confusing politics. There were so many questions he'd like to ask this man about his own opinions. Was he hoping the Confederacy would turn things around? Were there other reasons besides gratitude that had led him to give up his slaves before being forced to? He dared not ask more, even if he had to wonder forever.

Aunt Molly set a huge piece of blackberry pie in front of her former master. "Thank you kindly," he said as he sank his fork into the flaky crust. "In the last two years, many, many of us in Missouri have changed our minds about slavery," he explained, as if reading Joshua's mind. "In fact, the majority now favor emancipation." He glanced at the boy and smiled. "What helped changed *my* mind were some long conversations with your father."

Eliza surveyed the faces of her guests, all listening intently. "Our servants have no reason to leave. We love them like family, and they know it." She was smiling, too—first at Aunt Molly, then at Pete, and finally at Jim, who stood in the corner. "Right, Aunt Molly?" she asked as she turned back to the cook.

"Yes, Miz Eliza," came the reply.

As he watched their stone faces, Joshua wondered if the Wornalls knew their servants as well as they thought.

Billy had scarcely swallowed his first big bite of pie when he blurted out two questions, one behind the other. "Mr. Wornall, do you expect to be going off to war soon? Or do you have to hide in the woods like my father?"

"William Luke Carter!" Lucy exclaimed. Billy gulped and held his breath. Hearing Ma speak his full, official name was never a good sign.

His big brother was mortified, more so as he looked across the table. Billy's deep purple lips were coated with frothy whipped cream.

"Those are fair questions, Lucy," Mr. Wornall said, kindly, "and he deserves an answer." He turned to his young inquisitor, and addressed the boy as if he were his equal.

"There are many ways to get an exemption from military service, Billy," he replied. Immediately, he rose. "I hope we all get a good night's sleep, for tomorrow our family must get out of Jackson County, same as everyone else. We do need our rest."

With supper finished, everyone darted out for another game of baseball. Everyone except for Billy and his mother, that is.

"Remember that children, as guests, are to be seen and not heard," Joshua overheard her saying as she trudged up the stairs behind her son. It was one nineteenth-century rule the Carter children hadn't had much opportunity to learn, having spent little time being guests at anyone's table besides the Mullins—and *never* at a table as formal as this one.

By the time Ma released her captive, it was too dark to play ball. To make matters worse, he had to endure the gloats from the Mullins sisters as they passed him in the yard.

"You're just in time," Grandpa informed him, pointing in the direction of the well where his other grandsons and Frank were already heading. "There are three big washtubs full of water out here," he explained. "A community guest bath, you might say. I even got your clean clothes for you. Jump in and start washing."

"Aw! Grandpa, do we *have* to take a bath? " Billy groaned. Couldn't blame the boy. The Carters had just bathed three days ago, same as they did every Saturday night.

"Might be a good idea unless you plan to sleep on the floor," replied Grandpa. "Mrs. Wornall's white sheets will be coal black if you get in bed with those feet."

If Billy had any more questions, he didn't have time to ask. His able-bodied grandfather took advantage of the opportunity for a little fun. Grabbing his grandson by the waist, he heaved him over the side of the nearest washtub, clothes and all.

"I think you started something." Sam roared as Frank, fully-clothed, gleefully jumped in to join Billy. Tom and Joshua followed close behind, making use of the third tub.

"Do you think they might use a little soap?" asked Sam.

"Only if forced to," claimed Grandpa, chuckling. He handed one big bar of lye soap to Billy and another to Joshua. "Do a good job, boys, unless you want *me* to scrub you," he advised. The soap was soon in full motion as Grandpa climbed into the tub Mr. Mullins had just vacated.

The grass was soaked by the time they'd finished their water fights. Frank led the way up to the stranger rooms, taking two at a time. Normally, he slept upstairs near the rest of his family, but Grandpa assured his parents that as long as Frank could put up with his snoring, he was welcome to share the big bed that he and Tom had already claimed. The boys were overjoyed, and Grandpa was too tired to be bothered by any trouble they might cause.

Joshua, the last of the six, wasn't in a hurry at all. He was wishing the day might go on and on when he suddenly felt a hand on his shoulder. He jumped.

"I didn't mean to startle you, Joshua."

Embarrassed he turned to face Mr. Wornall. "After spending a night worrying about bushwhackers and jayhawkers, I guess I'm still a little nervous," Joshua explained.

As it turned out, the Wornalls wanted to let him know about the books upstairs in a basket. Sometimes guests left a book, sometimes took one. The boys were free to take any they liked.

Instantly, Joshua knew which one he wanted. His father had talked about reading it last year right here in this room, and he'd spotted it before ever going out to play baseball. It was *Uncle Tom's Cabin*. When published back in 1852, it had stirred up tremendous support for the cause of abolition. Though banned in the South, it soon became a best seller elsewhere.

Joshua had even noticed a page about it in his father's treasure box. The date was December 30, 1862, so this meant he'd made that entry right here, as well. "Things I want to remember about Harriet Beecher Stowe's book, *Uncle Tom's Cabin*" he'd written at the top of the page.

Back upstairs, Joshua pressed the book against his chest, as he stood looking out the window, enjoying a slight breeze. What a magnificent day this had been! Just imagine Pa reading this same book in this very room!

With his four roommates already asleep, he lit the oil lamp beside the soft chair and began reading as fast as he could, skimming parts of the book, knowing he'd come back to it later. He rushed on and didn't stop for two hours, when he finally discovered that the slave mother, who had been frantically running from hunters who were pursuing her, finally succeeded in getting to safety with her young son. She did it by carrying him in her arms across a frozen river.

Yawning, he lowered the wick of the lantern. Just as the flame was extinguished, it dawned on him--the slave mother's name was Eliza, same as Mrs. Wornall. Maybe he'd ask her tomorrow if she'd read the book. If so, he'd like to know what she thought of it. Or, considering how Billy had already asked enough questions, perhaps he would just wonder.

Learn much more about "Uncle Tom's Cabin" by reading a short version of the story. It's available as a free e-book at:

http://utc.iath.virginia.edu/childrn/cbcbmada1t.html

19

It would be years before Joshua heard the entire story of what transpired in the parlor next morning before he was even out of bed.

Grandpa and Mr. Wornall were looking at the latest edition of *Harper's Weekly* when Sam walked in. "It was all I could do to keep from laughing," Sam always said as he told the story.

The scene was quite comical. It was also beautiful. There Homer sat in a clean shirt, with his raggedy pants, and old gnarled, bare feet beneath the table. Sitting beside him, Mr. Wornall in his fancy suit, white shirt, tie, and shiny shoes, neither man seeming to notice they were anything but equal.

"Until the war started," Mr. Wornall was saying to Homer, "I managed to make a living from my five hundred acres of farmland. Nowadays, planting crops in Missouri is almost a useless endeavor. I've only put in a hundred acres this year."

Sam glanced at Homer. Eleven years of being next-door neighbors, it was easy for the two to have a meeting of the minds without saying a word. In this case, they were equally amused. Like most Missouri farmers, Cyrus Carter and Sam Mullins only had one-hundred and sixty acres each. The Carters had planted fifteen in 1862, just two this year.

"This morning, I have an important meeting in Kansas City—a real estate deal," John explained to Sam and Homer a few minutes later. "This means I'm going to need a lot of help to get us moved, considering how I took the whole day off to play and enjoy your fine company yesterday."

"Sam and I can help. And the older boys, too," offered Homer. "Then, we'll be on our way."

Mr. Wornall nodded amicably. "That's the way it works. You're on my team; I'm on yours."

He handed the September 5 edition of *Harper's Weekly* to Sam, pointing to a large drawing of the raid on Lawrence, now more than two weeks past. "They call that a raid? Heck, I call it a massacre!" Sam exclaimed after examining the article filled with horrible stories.

"Seems they did a fine job of the write-up, got it out quickly, too," said Mr. Wornall. "But I heard a prediction recently. Some say we'll soon be getting this kind of news coverage the day after a story occurs."

"Won't that be something? In my day, we only had letters to rely on, and those could take months to just get across Tennessee," stated Homer.

Abruptly, John Wornall turned toward the dining room. "Is that Lucy's voice I hear?"

"Yes, and Olivia's here, too," Lucy's voice rang out. The two entered the parlor.

"We were just talking about the day ahead," John Wornall said to the women. "Sam and Homer have signed all of you up to help us move. With everyone pitching in to get the first load over to the new place....and provided I get my work done.... I think we can be back here in time for a late lunch." There were nods all around.

"I was also saying that I was awake for hours last night, thinking about what I want to see us accomplish *after* we satisfy General Ewing's orders. Do you remember what I suggested yesterday as you stepped out of the carriage, Lucy?" he asked.

Lucy laughed. "Yes. You offered to pay a fortune for Old Nelly."

"Well, if you'll just give me that old mule and cart, I can arrange it so nobody has to sleep on the ground another night."

Lucy laughed out loud. "So what do you have in mind, Mr. Wornall?" she asked.

"Steamboats and trains," he answered, matter-of-factly. "As for the mule, I'll give her, as a gift, to Jim."

Sam guffawed. "Gift, you say? Better first put a red ribbon and bell 'round her neck so Jim can keep up with her."

Their host, though grinning, hardly stopped for a breath. "I studied the route to Salem last night. You can be there in less than a week, maybe as little as four days, depending on connections. How does that sound?" His head moved slowly, side to side as he surveyed the room for reactions.

Homer's came immediately. "Sounds like a wonderful deal to me," he said, looking at his daughter-in-law.

Lucy nodded. Though initially speechless, her broad smile spoke volumes.

"Mr. Wornall, the children would be thrilled," she eventually said, "and we'd all arrive rested, ready to start a new life." Her eyes turned toward Olivia, who seemed only to be studying the plush, red fabric on the seat of her husband's chair.

Sam shifted awkwardly while everyone else sat waiting.

"That's very generous of you, Sir," he told their kind benefactor when he finally found his voice, "but I've read a few stories of disasters on the water....sandbars, underbrush, guerrilla attacks, and ambushed trains sending passengers to their deaths. I think I'd rather go by wagon. That way we can take all the animals.... except for the mule, of course." Everyone laughed.

With eyes locked, Mr. and Mrs. Mullins smiled at one another agreeably.

"Well, I suppose I've been influenced by Cyrus much too long. I'll probably be as nervous as an old settin' hen, but I'm willing to risk public transportation," declared Lucy.

"Very well. Then, I have two good horses to spare," John said to Sam, without a moment's hesitation. "Added to your two, they could come in handy up north.... Lightening the load should be easy. With less travel time and fewer mouths to feed, you won't need nearly as much food. And you can put anything you don't need for the trip into trunks for Carters to carry on the steamboats and trains. They can stay around here and let you get a head start so you can be in Iowa to meet them when they get off the train at their final stop."

Their new travel planner was far from finished. "Now, while you are thinking about all that, we have three other problems to solve, the most immediate being where you will sleep tonight," he continued. "We won't be set for company yet. However, Eliza's parents, Rev. Thomas Johnson and wife Sarah, have a house twice the size of this one. Place isn't far from here."

He rambled on. "I'll ride to their farm early this afternoon, so we'll know by the time I get back for a late lunch if Thomas is agreeable." He glanced at Eliza, now standing in the doorway. "Say, we have lunch around two?" he asked.

She nodded agreeably.

He moved on: "From what I hear around town, it's already getting cool in Iowa. In fact, it could freeze there any day now. Joshua tells me the bushwhackers left you with few covers, no shoes, and little clothing. Eliza and her mother love the fine shops in Kansas City. Plus, Eliza's father has a large supply store where most folks stop before hitting the Santa Fe Trail or boarding a steamboat. So we'll have you ready for your first winter in Iowa before you leave here."

By now, Lucy was crying tears of joy. "Thank you so much," she managed to say.

"Lucy, I would do anything for Cyrus and his family. Maybe you don't realize that he's like a brother to me. I owe him a lot."

"You owe *him*?" Lucy exclaimed through her tears. "He's the one who owes you."

"No, what I owe him can't be replaced with dollars and cents, Lucy," he insisted. "Cyrus made my heart soften, just being around him. That was his gift to me. He challenged me to be more compassionate, helped me look closer at the difficulties of our nation and this awful rebellion, too. From what I've observed since yesterday, I believe much of how he thinks comes from his father." He looked at Homer, then at Sam. "It also has to do with his good Quaker neighbor. So, I think I owe a lot to both of you."

He took a deep breath and closed his eyes for a moment as if he was about to say a prayer. "Finally, regarding Cyrus....." He spoke slowly, as if looking for the perfect words. "Most of all, I want to do all I can to learn what happened to him. If he's been captured, we need to know where he's being kept. I'm working on a plan," he promised. "Tomorrow, I hope we have some answers."

Eliza spoke from the doorway. "Breakfast is getting cold, John."

Learn more about why Mr. Mullins might have had good reason to fear travel by steamboat by visiting

http://www.uni.edu/iowahist/Frontier_Life/Steamboat_Hints/Steamboat_Hints2.htm

20

Fortunately, for Joshua and everyone else at the breakfast table, he'd just swallowed the last bite of pancake when Mr. Wornall commenced talking. 'Cause that boy's mouth flew wide open the minute he heard the news about steamboats and trains. Just a half hour earlier, he'd dreaded getting out of bed, thinking how he'd be sleeping on the road again for the next two weeks.

Then, while he was still trying to absorb the excitement, Mr. Wornall abruptly switched topics. Yet he spoke with uncharacteristic hesitancy.

"Joshua, I'm wondering….could you possibly …. Uh, I have a big request of you. ….How would you feel about helping Jim and Pete load one of the wagons today?"

"I'd love to!" Joshua blurted out. Quickly, he covered his mouth. Mr. Wornall looked startled, perhaps not understanding the boy's reaction.

His mother certainly understood. He was certain of that. She'd heard him talk since he was a small child about how he'd love to find ways to make friends with some of the slaves in their neighborhood. He'd simply had no opportunity. In fact, his parents warned it could be dangerous for the slaves if he did—even dangerous for him, since he might be suspected of encouraging slaves to run away.

"Most slave masters are as fearful as their slaves are. Masters fear having to care for themselves because they've never done so," his father explained. "Well, it's not the slaves' fault. They didn't ask for this. Neither did their ancestors."

While white children, were isolated and guarded for their *own* protection, slaves were isolated and guarded, too, Cyrus said. Not for the slaves' protection, though—but because slave masters were "protecting their property," as they often put it. Of course, the real protection was for masters, who were actually protecting their privileged status above all.

For this reason, even small slave children were forbidden by their parents to talk to any white person except for those they were certain the master approved of. Ignoring this rule could result in severe beatings—or even worse, being sold and separated from loved ones. Slave masters used such ways to keep slaves from cooking up schemes, getting help to escape. Lately, with more and more slaves running off, slaves were more "protected" than ever.

Whites could also be falsely accused of helping runaways. So it was hard for slaves to get to know outsiders and learn from them, as well as for white people outside the slave system to learn from slaves or hear what they thought.

Joshua frequently thought of something his father said one day, back in the classroom: "Before folks can trust one another, they have to become friends."

Now, as servants rather than slaves, would Jim and Pete be less afraid to talk? He hoped so. He definitely needed some new friends.

In spite of the bright sunshine outdoors, it was dark in the musty-smelling cabin--so dark, Joshua stopped to let his eyes adjust when he first entered. The shutters were partially closed on their one window, located near the door, which faced west so the whole place was dismally dark.

"This is where we live," Jim said. "And here's what we have to move," he added, pointing out each item nearby. "There's the little table, three stools, one big box of dishes, Pete's little toy box from Master Frank, the iron pot, Mammy's flat iron, four quilts, bed sheets, our three pillows and two mattresses. Pete already put all our clothes in this big knapsack."

Joshua's eyes weren't the only thing having to adjust. From what he'd just heard, Jim and Pete must both be Aunt Molly's sons. He would never have guessed. Pete was so light-skinned he could pass for white, while Jim was as dark as Aunt Molly.

"So you two are brothers?" he asked, incredulously.

"Sure are. Guess nobody took time to 'splain that to you," Pete answered.

So where was their father--or fathers? He dared not ask, but hoped to find out before the day was over.

After standing in the cabin a few minutes, Joshua could see clearly. The family had one large, rectangular room with a partition running halfway across one end to provide some privacy for whoever might be sleeping on the other side. He was surprised to find that the two boys and their mother had almost as much space as the Carter family. A large fireplace, extending across half the back wall, had a big ledge for sitting or working. On cold winter nights, it must be quite cozy, he thought. The thick brick walls made it feel cooler than he expected now in the heat. A long counter, with one open shelf beneath it lined the wall on one side of the fireplace. Across the room sat a little table and three backless stools. There were two beds, about four feet wide. The heads were against opposite walls on each end of the cabin. The mattresses, already folded, lay near the foot of each bed.

"Me and Jim sleep here, Mammy over in that bed," Pete explained, pointing around the half wall.

"Will we be taking the bedposts?" Joshua asked. Jim and Pete laughed as if this was the funniest thing they'd ever heard.

"Not unless you want to spend the day pouring water on the floor so you can dig them up," Jim replied.

Joshua was soon laughing at his own foolishness.

"Those poles were put into the mud long before we came,

back when the floor was set," Jim explained.

"Guess you don't have to worry about thieves making off with it," Joshua said before telling how his own disappeared.

"Oh, we know 'bout bushwhackers!" cried Pete. "Just last February, they tried to string Mr. Wornall from the top balcony out front the house."

"Don't start that story, Pete. We'll never finish loading this wagon," warned Jim. "Save it until we're riding over to the new place. It's already seven o'clock. Gotta hurry. " He turned to Joshua: "It's a good story, but no better than the one about the Jayhawkers' visit. That was a close call for Mr. Wornall, too. They stayed three weeks and tore up eve'thing."

"That's all from our place. Matilda loaded her own things early this morning. Looks like we got plenty more room," Pete said, peering into the bed of the wagon.

"We'll have a lot less when we get through loadin' Han's things," sighed Jim as he pointed at another house, past the barn.

Joshua soon saw what Jim meant. Though a single man, Hans had as much as the other four combined. Was his pay more? Or had he managed to save through the years when his co-workers weren't paid at all? Either way, the difference was striking.

With Han's things loaded, Joshua stood staring into the wagon. The five servants owned twice what the Carters now did. Yet, if Mr. Wornall's plans worked out, Carters would have three times as much by the time they left for Iowa. What a contrast to most people now leaving Jackson County!

"So do you think the new place will have beds like the ones here?" he asked as they heaved a couple of steamer trunks from the big house to the wagon.

"If it has any beds at all, I 'spect so," answered Pete. "Never saw a slave bed any different."

"But we don't have to have beds," Jim assured him. "Our feather mattresses, even if we have to sleep on the floor, are much better than most slave mattresses. The usual ones are stuffed with scratchy straw. Most slaves are us'ly too tired to much notice."

As Joshua eased one of the soft-cushioned, parlor chairs into a corner of the wagon, wedging it in with the trunks before carefully covering it with a blanket, things seemed to fall into place in his head. Meager furnishings weren't the worst part of slave life, just as having to sleep on the bare floor had become only a minor irritation for him lately in the midst of all the other worries.

21

"Right there's where it happened, Joshua," Pete said, as they followed the other three wagons from the barn through the yard to the main road, where the Carters had first turned into the property yesterday.

"I'd already run over yonder," His index finger traced a line from a tiny sycamore near the fence on the far west of the property to the railing above the columns. "Saw the who-o-ole thing from behind that tree."

Joshua looked where Pete was pointing. He tried to imagine the ghastly sight of Mr. Wornall standing under the lovely, white railing with a rope around his neck. He wondered what it must have been like for Frank, witnessing all of this.

"The family had just left for church 'bout an hour earlier.... dressed nice and fine. Bunch o' men stopped 'em right 'fore they got to the first bend in the road," Pete explained. Leaning around Joshua, he looked at his brother questioningly. "How many men was it, Jim?"

"'Bout a dozen," Jim replied. "Now, don't forget to 'splain the part 'bout the uniforms."

Pete nodded. "What had 'em all fooled was these men all in blue, like Union soldiers." It was Joshua's turn to nod. He knew what that meant. The bushwhackers were always taking uniforms from dead soldiers, using them as disguise to get into places where they might be unwelcome otherwise. It would be too late by the time their victims realized who they were.

"Everybody was fooled, that is, 'cept Hans," Pete continued. "Fortunately, he was watchin' the road. Soon as he saw they'd all turned 'round, he got a mighty stro-o-ong hunch 'bout those bandits. ...took off, fast as light'ning t'where he knew there was a troop of *real* Union soldiers. Ol' Major Thatcher, a friend of Mr. Wornall, was in command."

"But the family had no idea a rescue was in the makin'," Jim interrupted. "Mr. Wornall fell into a heap of trouble, trying to convince them he didn't have no money buried on the place. Truth is—Mr. Wornall has safer places than most to keep his money. The bushwhackers 'fused to believe any rich man would be fool enough to get separated from his money. So they was throwin' fits and cursin' po' Mr. Wornall."

"Then, suddenly, Master Frank come 'round the corner, carryin' his little, double-barreled pistol that Mr. Wornall gave him." Pete laughed and went on with the story. "That gun's never loaded... didn't matter to Master Frank. He was tryin', of course, to think of anything to keep 'em from carryin' out their threats to kill his pa. So, he come 'round the southeast corner of the house with that shotgun pointed right at the enemy. Two of them suckers grabbed the gun right out of his hand and commenced to slap him 'round, over and over, 'til his little face was covered with welts."

Joshua, now holding his breath, just listened. They were speaking of the same boy who'd boldly walked up to him on the road yesterday, the boy who loved baseball and water fights. He'd been through a lot for a seven-year-old. Joshua thought of his missing father and how frustrating it was, not knowing where to even look for him. Yet Frank couldn't have done a thing for his father, standing right there in the front yard. Perhaps that felt even worse.

"Where were you and Aunt Molly? What about Matilda?" Joshua asked Jim.

"Bein' Sunday, it was our day off. So Matilda was over visiting her fellow at Mr. Bent's place up the road. Those two were sittin' side by side, in fact, when Hans went scurrying past to find the army," Jim said. "As for our ma, she was hiding her eyes in her apron, sittin' near the door of our place, tremblin'. Ever' once in a while I'd see her look up, then, quickly put her head back down, wailing louder than ever." He stopped for a deep breath before continuing. "As for me, I was hunched over behind Mammy's bed. 'Cause I just knew, when they finished with Mr. Wornall, they'd come lookin' for any of us to take off and sell." Joshua wondered if the same look of terror now crossing Jim's face had crossed his face during the moments he was recalling.

"They don't care 'bout families," cried Jim. He gazed at the clouds as if he was seeing something far, far away—or perhaps long, long ago.

Joshua wasn't prepared for what happened next. First, Jim handed him the reins, then unbuttoned his shirt, wadded it up, and used it to cover his eyes. Leaning over to rest his head in both his hands, he sobbed for several minutes as the well-trained horses clip-clopped down the road.

Driving was effortless, but Joshua wasn't as experienced as Jim. Only once did he take his eyes off the horses. That's when he saw the thick, striped scars across Jim's shoulders.

"Bet he's thinkin' of the last time he saw his father, the day 'fore the three of us got bought by Mr. Wornall," offered Pete. "Our three sisters and Jim's father were all sold in one day...all to separate slave holders."

Now facing forward, elbows on knees, Jim squinted as if doing so would somehow help his memory. "Mammy always says it's not my fault, but I will go to my grave thinkin' it was."

Waiting patiently, Joshua steered the horses around a corner, onto a brick street.

"Our family was havin' a hard time with the ole, cruel master over in Kentucky; but we was together," Jim continued, sobbing again. "If a family's together, troubles can be borne a heap of a lot easier." He paused. "It was my talkin' back to the overseer got us all in trouble. I couldn't pull that old sack of cotton any further. It was just too heavy, so I told him I needed to go empty it. When he called me a lazy fool, I spat on the ground and called him a tyrant. It was a terrible mistake," he said."He had me by the scruff of my neck going straight to the master 'fore I knew it. ... I knew full well the cat o' nine tails was next, though....that's what the ole master always used. He did his own whippin', too—not like most who hired somebody else to do the job. He took the word of the overseer. Always seemed the master harbored within him a demon he needed to unleash, and that's what he did. I was his excuse that day, but it didn't stop with the beating."

He reached for a corner of his shirt and quickly wiped more tears away. "No sir, it didn't stop there," he repeated. "Ol' man wasn't satisfied. Told me he'd had enough of my family always mouthing off....it was the first I realized, but Mammy said later Pappy and my two older sisters had given him plenty to think about ove' the last two years, too. That's why they'd got all the beatings I knew 'bout already." He stopped and sighed. "So she's prob'ly right—it wasn't really my fault, but when a nine-

99

year-old boy talks like I did to an overseer, the maste' has a way of makin' him feel responsible for a long time to come.....guess 'twas a worse offense to the maste' than a grown man sassin'."

Pete smiled and took over from there. "Ol' master never knew what he'd sold, though, when he sold Mammy to Mr. Wornall."

"Neithe' did Mr. Wornall know what he'd bought," Jim added, joining his brother's laughter.

Pete nodded. "Only Mammy knew. Seven months later, I come along. Mr. Wornall said I be the best free gift he eve' got. I never knew my sisters or my pa, of course. Hard to miss somebody you neve' knew, though I do live with the sadness of Jim and Mammy ever' day. I hear 'em talkin' and cryin' 'bout all the others, so I do my best to comfort 'em."

Jim had composed himself, but Joshua fought hard to hold back his own tears as they pulled onto Wornall's new land.

"Is this it?" he asked, puzzled. "I heard Mr. Wornall say the house is on Main Street," he said. "Still looks like we're in the country, the way these houses are so far apart."

"Things will change," Jim replied. "They always do."

22

"Not only have we got beds," Jim yelled to the other two from the doorway of the new quarters, we've got ourselves a cement floor." Joshua and Pete ran to see. "This is a *modern* cabin....even got two full rooms." Jim sounded excited. "Just one problem, though."

"What's that?" asked Joshua.

"The walls of this place are wood—they'd burn to the ground as fast as you could say 'skip-to-my-Lou'. Never know when somebody's gonna set a torch to things these days." He shrugged, put down the mattress he was carrying, and rushed back to the wagon for another load.

When they were done, Hans pulled out a big jug of water and a sack of enormous, fluffy biscuits, more tender than any Joshua had ever tasted.

"Aunt Molly's lemon tea biscuits," explained Hans. "She found a way of makin' bread so nobody need spend a half hour beating the dough. The secret is lemon juice."

"Lemon juice? What's a lemon?" asked Joshua. Pete laughed and proceeded to answer.

"It's a fruit. You never seen it?" Joshua, a bit embarrassed at his ignorance, said nothing.

"We get all kinds of rare things here 'cause of the Santa Fe Trail," continued Pete. "Sometimes Rev. Johnson gets lemons in his store and brings 'em over to Miz Eliza."

"Do they grow around here?" Joshua wanted to know.

"Oh, no!" Hans chimed in. "They need lots of sunshine. A lot of what comes up on the trail originates down in Mexico. Traders bring lots of food items and many other fine goods up to Santa Fe and get good money for it."

"I once heard Miz Johnson tell Miz Eliza that some of those goods go all the way to the east coast of the United States and on to Europe!" exclaimed Jim.

"Aunt Molly says we should soon be getting something called 'baking powder' here, too," added Hans. "Says 'twill make baking revolutionary. Guess we're in for lighter cakes and nice, tasty, flaky biscuits without the need for lemons or all the necessary beatin'. Chances are it will come from back east, though, 'stead of Mexico. They've already had baking powder in England for years. Probably would have here except the only powder folks are thinkin' 'bout these days in America is *gunpowder*."

"Billy will sure be glad to hear that!" Joshua declared. "Ma'll be glad, too. I'm sure she'll find plenty of other things to keep him busy besides beatin' biscuits every morning."

"Yes, we should see some amazing things if folks ever figure out how to stop being savages," Homer Carter agreed.

While the men made themselves comfortable in the shade, Pete drew a large circle in the dirt. Next, he pulled a small bag with a drawstring from his little box of toys. From the bag, he extracted two dozen marbles of various colors, placing them in the center of the circle. Outside the circle he carefully spaced five shooters. "Come on," he called, motioning to the other boys. "Let's all play."

Pete won by a long shot. With the marbles back in the bag, he pulled out a book Joshua immediately recognized. It was from a set of *McGuffey's Readers*. Pa had used these books to teach scores of children besides his own, as had many educators across America since 1830. Most teachers liked McGuffey because he was also a minister who encouraged character building in his stories.

"How far have you gotten?" Frank asked Pete.

"I'm almost done with the whole reader," replied Pete. "Read it without any help from anybody."

This startled Joshua. Either Pete had learned exceptionally fast or Frank had started teaching him long before his father had granted their freedom. Had he done so with his father's approval? Either way, Frank could have gotten in big trouble, for teaching a slave to read was against the law.

"I like the story about the father whose wife left him to care for their baby while she ran an errand."

Joshua noticed that Pete suddenly spoke exceptionally clear and slow without the slang he'd used all morning. Though two years Frank's elder, he appeared desperate to please his teacher.

"Yes, Pete," Frank answered. "And do you remember what happened soon as the man's wife left?"

"Sure do ... He left, too, because a messenger came to say the king wanted him in the palace right away. He was afraid to say no to the king."

"You learned well." Frank spoke as if Pete were a small child and he an adult.

"Next, a snake entered. He was about to bite the baby," Pete continued. "The dog saw. He killed the snake to save the baby. The man got home. He saw blood on the dog's mouth and decided straight away that dog killed the baby. So the man killed the dog."

"Very good, Pete. What happened when he got inside? "

"He saw he'd made a very big mistake since the snake was dead and the baby fine. Soon his wife returned. He told her what happened and begged her not to scold him, for he already felt bad. She forgave him, but reminded him that shame and repentance always must follow thoughtless behavior."

Pete stopped, looked at his teacher, and asked, "How did I do?"

"You did well," commended Frank. "I think you understood the whole story."

"Yes, I understood it very well," replied Pete. "That man made me think of the old master who left marks on Jim's back and sold our family members off to distant plantations. As far as I know, old master never had no shame nor repentance at all."

"I see," said Frank as he reached for another tea biscuit.

*****

"You never did tell me where Mrs. Wornall was when her husband got strung from the balcony," Joshua said to Pete as they pulled out on the road again.

"Holding her baby girl in her arms, she stood at the window and screamed at those bush-whackers like they all were little boys needing a scolding. Soon they came in and went room to room, loading everything they liked into three wagons out front, along with several of Mr. Wornall's best horses. Lord only knows what they would have gotten if Hans hadn't summoned the soldiers."

"If they hadn't got what they did, I doubt we could ever get it moved in one day," declared Joshua. Jim laughed until he had tears running down his cheeks.

"Rich folks got their own troubles," he said before long. "They's got lots more needs than po' folks. Ain't that right, Pete?"

"True 'nuf, Jim. Like Doc Jennison. ... Real soldiers can manage with just a tent--not Jennison, though. He had to have Mr. Wornall's who-o-o-le parlor for *his* headquarters."

Joshua knew other stories about the infamous Doc Jennison, but had no idea this vicious Jayhawker had once taken over the Wornall place. "What happened?" he asked.

"Jennison came last year, right after ya' pa left our place. Little Sallie Wornall was jest three weeks old," Jim replied. "Two hundred of Jennison's men camped on Wornall's lawn eight days while Doc lived in luxury like the place was his own. Those ruffians tore up all the fences and ate every animal on de' place. Worst of all, Mr. Wornall thought sure old Jennison was gonna kill him. He threatened to almost ever' day he was there 'cause he was shoah Mr. Wornall was aiding the Confederacy. Miz. Wornall kept sayin' the only thing would save 'em was the Master—the one up yonde', that is." He pointed to the sky.

"'Twas Frank who charmed those guys," Pete added. "It was right funny. One of them liked him so much, they traded knives, left Pete with the bette' one—on *purpose*."

"That's what's so strange 'bout dealing with troublemakers," Jim declared. "Sometimes one of 'em gets a soft spot in his ole' hard heart." He turned to Joshua. "Shoa happened with Doc Jennison. He ended up apologizing to Mr. Wornall before they all left. According to Hans, he even gave Mr. Wornall $2500 for damages."

About a mile before they got back to the country home, Joshua posed the question he'd wanted to ask all day. "Jim, how has life changed now that you are a hired hand and not a slave?"

"Besides havin' a little money in my pocket?"

Joshua nodded.

"Hm-m-m. Guess it's mostly in my mind. I live in the same house, do the same work for as many hours as before. It's just good knowin' I can leave if I decide to, with or without my family, if need to. Nobody else's gonna sep'rate us from one another' agin. Knowin' that, I sleep a whole lot bette', too." He cleared his throat and once again took on a far-off look.

"Mr. Wornall has been very kind to us," he finally said. "He's allays tell us he love us like his own children, but I'm not so sure. To me, he's still my maste'. Maybe I'll always feel that way. Maybe it's just in my head. Right now, I b'lieve it's bette' for us to stay, but those freedom papers ... they's bigger than all Mr. Wornall's treasures.

"Times are changing fast, though. People change, too. We just all change slowly, no matter what color of skin we got." He ceased talking as if he'd said his piece, led the horses over to the watering trough, and dashed into the kitchen to help his mother with the fried chicken.

Back home, Joshua was always helped with the cooking, especially if there was chicken to fry. Surely Aunt Molly could put him to work here, too—at least with sampling. Lucy Carter had *other* plans for her son.

"You are a guest, and I don't think Aunt Molly needs any more hands in the kitchen," she insisted. "Now, skedaddle up to your room. Gather your things." She pointed to an open trunk on the porch beside her. "Put your knapsack here with the others. Yesterday's clothes are laid out on your bed, all clean and ironed, thanks to Aunt Molly."

No need arguing with Ma. "If need be," Pa always said. "She could stand up to any general."

It's time now to go to

http://**justfollowingorders.takecourage.org**

to hear the music you'll read about in the next chapter.

To **learn more** about what life for families in slavery, read an account by Harriett Ann Jacobs, written about her own family, at:

http://www.pbs.org/wgbh/aia/part3/3p477.html

23

It didn't take two minutes to pack. His extra clothes, a box of checkers, two school books, plus *Uncle Tom's Cabin* fit easily in his knapsack. That and Pa's tin box, now resting on the bedside table, were all he had to his name. That is, until he reached for the box and discovered the large stack of paper beneath it.

Lying next to the paper were a dozen newly-sharpened pencils, an eraser, and an envelope with his name on it and a note inside.

Dear Joshua,

Mr. Wornall told me about your treasure box. I thought you might add more pages to it.

Eliza Wornall

No need for him to stop and think about anything. He'd been thinking all morning, with his father's last entry for the box in the back of his mind all the while. Settling back into the armchair, he hurriedly wrote "Living for Peace" at the top of the first sheet of paper. On the next line, he added the wise words Jim had spoken only minutes earlier.

"Times are changing fast. People change, too. But we all change slowly." Jim

It was something else he wanted never to forget.

Now he was ready to fill several pages with Jim and Pete's stories.

"Joshua, your mothe' wants to know what's keeping ya'." It was Jim, speaking from the doorway.

Joshua looked at his friend and nodded. "I'm coming, Jim, but first I need to know your last name. I want to write it down so I can remember it."

"It's Freedman," Jim answered proudly. "The day Mr. Wornall gave me my papers, showing I was my own man, I told him I wanted to change my name. He agreed 'twas a good idea. 'Fore that, I just used my ol' master's name, kept that one to-o-o long." He grinned before quickly taking leave.

"Freedman," Joshua echoed. "I like that." Jim never heard

the complement. He was already gone. So was Joshua, a half minute later, with all his belongings in tow.

Two steps past the landing, he heard his mother's high soprano voice, coming from somewhere near the front yard. How he'd missed her singing! She'd hardly sung at all since his father left for Lawrence.

What instrument was playing in the background? Brighter than Mr. Mullin's guitar or the church pump organ, the sound energized him. The song he'd heard once at a barn dance. Its words were strange, didn't fit the melody. Inviting people to "listen to the mockingbird," that was "singing o'er the grave" of a girl named Hally. It was deceiving, for it said that the girl was only sleeping.

He thought of Andrew. He wasn't sleeping; he was dead. In one way, he wanted to welcome the lie of the mockingbird tune. In another, he wanted to scream out the truth.

Dropping his belongings in the designated trunk, he rounded the same corner of the house as yesterday, and stepped onto the front porch, between the columns and right up to the massive exterior doors.

"I feel like one so forsaken" his mother was singing now. Maybe some people needed the half-truth of the second verse before coming to the last verse that gave the cold facts about what he'd been feeling since Sunday, same as he'd felt as it dawned on him that his father had disappeared.

He stood in the foyer, taking in the richness of the scene along with the music. The parlor, which he knew only from the rear door leading to the dining room, lay on the left. Six feet ahead, the gleaming staircase called him up to explore the wonders of rooms he'd never entered.

Turning toward the music, he encountered an enormous, chocolate brown, panel door. It had been pushed aside to allow entry to a room almost as large as the parlor. Yet he'd not seen this room before. Inside, his mother was singing the same song again as the smiling eyes of the two women locked.

Swiftly the hostess' hands flew across the keys of the beautiful square, but boxy, instrument that looked much like a small dining room table.

Olivia and Matilda stood next to one another in the far corner, swaying, while Jenny, Ednie, Betsy and Mary all danced gleefully. Sometimes the girls held hands and danced in a circle. Other times, the younger two would break away and twirl round and round until they staggered or fell. Then, a few seconds later, they'd rejoin the older girls, squealing with delight.

Meanwhile, the two babies stood, one on each side of the instrument, each pair of hands wrapped around one of the thick legs. Bouncing their padded bottoms up and down, they craned their necks to look into the face of Mrs. Wornall.

Still in the doorway, Joshua was stupefied. He wondered at the fingers, all seeming to know exactly where to go, as if they weren't even connected to the music maker. Slowly, he made his way inside, his own hands gliding carefully across the beautiful wood of the instrument. Next, he studied Mrs. Wornall's feet and the three pedals. She occasionally pressed one, sometimes two, one with each foot—effortlessly, he thought. She made it all look so easy.

How different from the church pump organ! In Mt. Pleasant, Mrs. Smith always needed a strong boy, sitting beside her on the bench, to move the pair of heavy pedals up and down alternately in order to keep a constant flow of air moving at just the right speed to produce the desired sounds.

"What does that word say?" he now asked as Mrs. Wornall stopped for a break.

"Steinway," said she. "It's German. Mr. Steinway built the first in New York ten years ago. No longer do Americans have to send to Europe for fine pianos. Want to try it out?"

Unfortunately, he never got a chance. As soon as Aunt Molly rang the dinner bell, the whole house was aflutter with everyone moving toward what Frank assured them was "the best fried chicken in all of Missouri."

24

"It's all arranged," Mr. Wornall told them as he reached for the steaming corn Joshua was passing his way. "Eliza's parents are ready and waiting for you. You'll join half a dozen other families already at their place because of the Order."

Nine families sleeping under one roof!

The host smiled at the shock registering on the face of his guests. "Don't worry," he said. "The Johnsons are hospitable folks. They'll have a room for each family and more to spare. I've suggested they could open a hotel, since all but one of their children is gone."

Mrs. Wornall, jovial as her husband, nodded approval.

He hardly paused. "So everything's settled. We'll hitch the

extra horses up for Sam and Olivia before we leave here and go unload the last of our things at the new place. I promise to have you at the Johnson's by nightfall." He cleared his throat—nervously, Joshua thought—before glancing at his wife.

"About Rev. Johnson.....An amazing man, he is...has accomplished a lot. The two of them came here when they were young and newly married. He's played roles on both sides of the current controversies, so it's sometimes difficult to know which side he's on.... Thomas....that's his given name... grew up believing the white man had all the answers for everyone, especially for Indians and slaves. Before statehood, as a politician, he did everything he could to keep Kansas from starting out as a free state. Generally, he gets his way. So when Kansas *did* enter as a free state, that was very hard for him. I thought I should probably forewarn you."

He turned to Lucy. "Thomas was here at this table several times with Cyrus. The two listened carefully to one another, too."

"Change hasn't come easily for Pa," Eliza cut in. "I don't guess it does for any of us."

Joshua noticed that her words were almost identical to Jim's. Had Jim been listening to the Wornalls? Or could it possibly be the other way around?

"It's sort of like practicing piano," she went on. "I had to do that every day, growing up. A person can practice long and hard for years and make improvement, but if something is practiced wrong, it's very hard to correct. The mistakes become habits, like second nature."

She had everyone spellbound. They weren't finished eating. Yet, for the moment, not a fork was in motion.

"Slavery happened because so many of us grew up selfishly thinking it was good, without stopping to think otherwise. To my father, it was something we were entrusted by God to practice.

It's hard for me to imagine now. That's how I was raised to think, though. Only in the last year or two have I started seeing slavery as an evil we dare not continue."

She shook her head slowly, side to side. "Slavery will destroy us all, but getting free from it won't be easy either." With eyes downcast, she sighed before plunging on. "I doubt my father will live long enough to come to that conclusion. Yet he's got a big heart and is liked by many—you'll see."

Joshua thought of the tin box and vowed, starting tomorrow, to keep a pencil and paper in his shirt pocket for moments like this.

The forks began flying again as Mr. Wornall picked up the dialogue. "Tomorrow morning, the Mullins can leave for Iowa," he said, looking at Sam. "I stopped to talk with a stagecoach driver this morning. He gave me a map of the safest, easiest roads up that way. Those north of the Missouri aren't as good as in Jackson County, so be careful." He passed a paper from his shirt pocket down the table.

"Thank you, but I thought you had business to take care of this morning," Sam said with a grin as he glanced at the map.

"Oh, I did that also. What's so grand about this young city—everything is close together, with our new home near most businesses. By the way, I ran into our old friends George and Sadie Miller this morning, Eliza. They'll be our new neighbors."

"Terrific!" exclaimed his wife.

"Joshua was telling me on the way here yesterday about their recent visit and the pledge to help find Cyrus. So George and I put our heads together." He finished one biscuit and reached for another as he turned his attention back to Lucy. "Since Eliza and her mother love to shop, I thought you three ladies could round up some nice things in the big city tomorrow morning. Then, in the afternoon, I'll take you and the two ministers to Union headquarters. We're gonna learn all we can about Cyrus' whereabouts before you start up the Missouri."

He looked at the cook, now clearing the table. "Thank you kindly, Aunt Molly."

The cook nodded back. Leaning into a slight bow, she smiled broadly. "Yes, Maste'."

The "master" wasn't finished. "And that brings us to the Carter's departure. On Friday, Homer and the boys will go to Johnson's Trading Post where we'll get you all outfitted for the winter ahead. So you could be ready to hop on a steamboat to St. Joe by Saturday, spend the weekend there, and catch the train to Hannibal first thing Monday morning. Now, in Hannibal, you'll be tired from the train trip. But you'll want to spend time watching ships come and go in the crowded port and exploring the banks of the mighty Mississippi. Once you've rested there for two nights, you should be ready for a long day on another steamboat, going all the way up to Burlington, Iowa. A night there and you can hop a train, back west. In only an hour, if all goes well, you should arrive in Mt. Pleasant, Iowa, the evening of September 19, a month earlier than you'd expected under the old plan. And, if all goes well with the Mullins, they'll be there waiting for you."

"Mr. Wornall, have you slept at all since we arrived?" Lucy cried. "How did you get everything worked out so quickly?"

"Details are his specialty," Eliza sighed. "Now, if we're ready for dessert, Aunt Molly and I came up with lemon meringue pie this morning."

Jim entered the room, a pie in each hand, while Pete placed a small bowl of lemons in front of Joshua along with a paring knife. "Want to try one?" he asked. "Mrs. Wornall says it was the favorite fruit of General Stonewall Jackson.

"That's right," Eliza confirmed. "Nobody knows where he managed to find them. His troops say he had one every single day 'til he died a week after being accidentally shot by one of them back in May. Rest his soul."

"He probably had good connections with South Carolina. They've got plenty of lemons down that way, I hear," added John.

Jim cut a big slice and handed it to Joshua before hastening to do the same for Homer and Sam. Eager to please, Joshua sank his teeth into the juicy pulp.

Jim and Pete, along with everyone at the table, had tears in their eyes, watching the puckering lips. Soon they were all laughing together.

"Jim is quite a prankster, but this should be a lot sweeter," Aunt Molly assured them as she placed a big slice of pie in front of the squint-eyed taste testers before serving the others.

"But I wasn't joking when I told you about Stonewall Jackson's habit," said Eliza.

"Must be those lemons that gave him his dogged determination," Homer suggested, chuckling. "If so, I wonder if I might get some lemons growin' in Iowa. Think we're gonna need all the determination we can get to deal with the winters there."

"I'm afraid you're out of luck on that one, Homer, but you're sure to have a fine corn crop there," Mr. Wornall said.

He looked at Tom. "I hear some folks around here like to sing, So soon as we're done eating, I'd like everyone to go back to the music room for a song one of our former slaves taught us."

He glanced at Jim, standing quietly in the corner of the dining room. "Would you please fetch Hans and tell him to bring his harmonica. I'd like you servants to all join us."

Apparently, Eliza knew what tune he wanted. She sat down at the piano and immediately played a brief, but lively, introduction as Hans skillfully wrapped his fingers around the tin of the tiny instrument and put his lips to the wood.

Tom was the only one *not* singing. Instead he comically

twisted and turned his lips to mimic Han's. Probably dreaming of a day when he might have his own harmonica, thought Joshua. That might be nice. Surely the noise couldn't be worse than the kid's singing.

One thing he knew for certain. "Ain't Gonna Study War No More" would soon be one of their family favorites. What a refreshing life it would be, studying anything besides war! The words would definitely be the next thing he'd put in the tin.

Learn more about how things got to the southern end of the

Santa Fe Trail by visiting:

http://www.caminorealheritage.org/camino/camino.htm

25

Joshua could hardly bear the thought of leaving Jim and Pete. The Wornall family had been wonderful. He knew his father loved them dearly. Yet it was those two boys he wanted to get to know better, more than all the others.

One question remained. So just ten minutes after they got back on the road going toward the city, he asked it. "Jim, did you ever think about where you'll go and what you'll do if ever you move away from the Wornall family?"

"That's *all* a man in slavery thinks about." Jim promptly replied. "Been askin' myself that question since long 'fore I got these stripes on my back. When a body's a slave, such thinkin' is just a'dreamin', though. Now I's free to go, it's more akin to plannin' when and how." He tilted his head slightly to get a glimpse of Joshua's face. "So is ya askin' if I got any plans?"

Joshua simply nodded encouragement, which was all Jim needed. "A free man don't mind talkin' plans if he's got a kind maste' like John Wornall. It don't matte' if Mr. Wornall gets word...' 'course you aren't lookin' to talk to him 'bout it.... anyway,.... I s'pose."

Joshua rapidly shook his head.

"Oh, no. I'm just asking like any good friend would do," he assured him.

Jim, apparently not too worried, plunged right in.

"Now, Mr. Wornall would let us go if we asked. It's jus' right now, it wouldn't be a good thing for us with Mammy being so old and attached here and me likely to get snatched up by either bushwhackers or jayhawkers. Hard to say what either might do. Good jayhawker might just give us a ride to Kansas, even help find me a job. No way of knowin' if it would be better than the job here, though, where we get ever'thin' we need. Now, as for the bushwhackers, they could easily sell us for fish bait if they chose. By that, I mean they don't care how much they get, cause we slaves are only worth what they can use us for, wheneve' they get a chance. So, it ain't smart for us to think of leavin' right now. We'd be out on the road, as bad off as you' family was yeste'day, e'en though we got papers sayin' we be free. Bushwhackers don' care *what* the papers say."

All this time, Pete sat perfectly still. Now, *he* had something to say. "Jim, you only got to the first of Joshua's question. At the rate you be going with all this talk, he's neve' gonna hear the most interestin' part 'bout where we might go and what we might do."

Jim nodded agreeably. He started again. "Some of it depends on you, little brothe'. If you would hurry and grow six more inches, you could easily pass for a man. Besides.... Lord knows, you'd have no trouble convincin' anybody you can cook. You've been raised in the kitchen, unlike me, who grew up a'workin' the fields."

"You're learning to serve food, though, since there ain't so much work in the fields these days," Pete interrupted before taking over the entire conversation.

"So, to answer your question, Joshua," says Pete. "Soon as I get tall enough to pass for a grown cook, I gonna start lookin' for a job." He sat up proudly. "It helps I can pass for white. That way, I can get more money."

It was Jim's turn. "Once Pete gets a job cookin', we think he could help me fin' a good job at some othe' rest'rant a'waitin' tables. We wouldn' eve' act like we in the same family, though. That way we would have more money comin' in from Pete's job so Mammy don't have to work no-o-o moa'. Now, soon as I get some money saved, I plan to travel." With his whole body bouncing to the rhythm of the reins, he got a faraway look again. Yet this time his eyes were much brighter, as if seeing the future instead of the past.

"You could come to Iowa and visit us," Joshua suggested. "I'm sure Ma wouldn't mind."

"'T'would be nice, Joshua," Jim returned. "But I'm going south."

"South? Why would any Negro want to go south?" asked Joshua.

"Cause he might have a girl down there," Jim answered without offering another word.

"A girl?" queried Joshua. "You got a girl down south?"

"Yep. Sho' do. She was livin' on the Bent place, where Matilda's got her manfriend. My girl's name is Adena. Mr. Wornall says it means 'adorned.' If so, it sho' fits her. She's the most beautiful girl I eve' saw, though I ain't seen her in a year. Ol' Mr. Bent took her to Sherman, Texas, sold her 'long with the rest of his slaves 'cause he was 'spectin' it wouldn't be long 'til the Union gonna free us all."

"Anything special about Sherman?" Joshua asked.

"Sho' is. Bushwhackers got a big camp there. Those Texans are real hospitable toward Confederates, so it's become one of the most popular places for Missourians in the whole country."

Once again, Jim looked very, very sad. "Adena an' me could have us a home now, as free people, if she was around. Cause of Order Number 9—that's the one that freed all Missouri slaves belonging to Confederates last month," he explained. 'Stead, Matilda lost her man-friend and I lost Adena at the same time. Matilda and I talk about us.... maybe someday...... go togethe' an' see if we can find 'em both, though folks tell us we just as well give up. Ain't no way a'knowin' if they be in Texas or Georgia or anywhere in b'tween by now." He stopped and hung his head. "Or if they both already got somebody else to love."

26

Joshua hadn't seen so many people in one place since the Battle of Lone Jack. No fighting here, though. It looked like a big family reunion. "Bet they're all Confederates," Grandpa cautioned. "Just keep quiet about politics and try to get along, boys."

Adults—most of them women—stood around visiting, holding babies of all sizes while at least twenty children, ranging from about five to fifteen, were playing Annie-Over. It was the favorite game of everyone at the Carter boys' old school. Cyrus loved playing, too. In fact, he was normally the first selected when teams were chosen.

While the game usually couldn't be played on a big two-story house, one end of the Johnson place was only one story tall, making it ideal.

"Ya'll come on in now," Rev. Johnson said as he held the back door open. "Make yourself right at home. Everybody else ate supper two hours ago, but Sarah's always got a pot of somethin' on the back of the stove. It's bean soup tonight with plenty of cornbread on the side."

Having been forewarned, Joshua wasn't shocked at the size of the house. It was *Rev. Johnson's* size that he couldn't get over. Why, Ma could make pants for all four of her sons from one pair of his overalls!

The simple supper was wonderful. It would have been even better, though, if he'd had a chance to share it with some boys his own age. To his disappointment, while eating, he watched as everyone outside filed indoors for the night.

Mrs. Johnson had a place set up for the women and children three tables away, but seated Joshua with the men. Billy looked at his brother enviously. Joshua grinned back.

As soon as the women and children finished supper, they left so the kids could go to bed. That meant Joshua could go sit alone in the dark or listen to the men talk. The way it turned out, sitting in the dark alone would have been less disturbing, but not nearly so interesting.

"So, Mr. Mullins," Rev. Johnson began. "Cyrus tells me you come from a Quaker family. You know, we actually had Quakers who ran an Indian mission school near the one I established. They didn't operate it quite like we did, though—thought they could teach the Indians white man's ways without converting them to Christianity. They even allowed them to sometimes speak their native tongue instead of English. That never works, I can tell you." Mr. Mullins offered no comment, but the minister wasn't comfortable with that. "You call yourselves 'Friends,' don't you, Sam?" he asked.

Joshua sighed. It was time to change the subject. He'd heard Quaker stories all his life, but this discussion wasn't anything like the ones along the Little Blue.

"Either name is acceptable." Mr. Mullins respectfully answered. "The name 'Friends' is important to us, though. We do our best to befriend everyone and try to respect the choices of others."

"Of course, that's the American way, isn't it?" The minister suddenly sounded almost reverent.

Mr. Mullins continued. "We don't have any Quakers living near us. So my wife and I join good folks like the Carters for worship when we can. We treasure our Quaker values, one being we believe slaves should enjoy the same freedom as anyone else."

"Oh, I see," Rev. Johnson said. Joshua assumed the man might be feeling quite uncomfortable, considering he still owned slaves. If so, he didn't show it. After a few minutes of silence between them, the quiz began again. "So I understand many Quakers believe slavery could be abolished *without* war?"

"Oh, we *know* it can be!" Sam Mullins replied. "Back before the Constitution was ever written, a Quaker by the name of John Woolman proved so."

Rev. Johnson's eyebrows shot up two inches, but Mr. Mullins continued without a pause. "Woolman was an itinerant minister. As he traveled, he made it a point to talk to Quakers who still owned slaves. Even though he detested slavery, he cared enough about the slaveholders to diplomatically tell them that slavery was harming them as much as the slave—in those days, that was a new thought. He even refused food prepared by slaves. His plan worked. All Quakers decided together that slavery should be denounced.... That's the Quaker way," he added. "We believe that, with respect, anyone can become reasonable in time."

"I'm sure you'll be happy living among Friends, up in Iowa, then. So how are Quakers handling this war, since they hate slavery and also refuse to take up arms? Must be quite a dilemma."

Sam Mullins nodded. "I'm not aware of any Iowa Friends who have taken up arms, though some Quakers back east have. Mostly, Friends have risked their lives helping slaves find freedom."

"Yes, I've heard a lot about their illegal operations on the 'freedom train,' as they like to call it," Rev. Johnson said with a hint of sarcasm. "At least they don't go out stealing other property or shooting slave holders like those abolitionists in Lawrence. It's too bad about what happened there, but they had it comin'. That town's full of troublemakers."

He glanced at each of his guests, as if imploring them to turn his monologue into a conversation. Getting no response, he continued: "It will be interesting to see what *Harper's Weekly* has to say about all this. They do a good job of telling both sides of the story. I expect folks will really be up in arms, once Harper's gets their version of the story out."

His stunned guests merely sat in silence. Obviously, he'd not seen the front of the most recent copy of *Harper's Weekly,* clearly showing citizens of Lawrence as victims of an atrocity.

Did Rev. Johnson really think all the people in Lawrence were killers and thieves? Perhaps he didn't know the family's connection to the city or how Cyrus had disappeared. If so, had he stopped to think how his words would strike Grandpa Carter? Whatever he knew, whatever he noticed in their faces—

for some reason he abruptly shifted his attention to Joshua.

"So what do you have to say about things here in Missouri, Joshua?"

The boy blinked and jerked his head, trying to absorb the sudden shift in conversation. Did he dare say what he knew with Grandpa's clear warning to steer clear of politics? What would Pa do at a moment like this?

He raised his head in confidence. "I'm hoping the Charcoals will get their way. Like them and my Aunt Charlotte over in Lawrence, I want to see slavery abolished as soon as possible in this state. I just wish everyone could have a long, peaceful conversation. Of course, if we have to settle for the Claybanks and wait for years before we see the last slaves freed, then that's better than the Snowflakes winning."

"For a lad who's hardly been out of Jackson County, I'd say you know quite a lot about politics," the minister offered when he finally stopped laughing. "Where did you learn all that?"

"Oh, I read the papers every chance I get," Joshua replied. He was telling the truth. No need to say "the papers" were clippings he'd seen just yesterday in his father's tin. "I know all about what President Lincoln proposed last year for ending slavery by compensating slave holders in Missouri," he went on. "If Missouri had agreed, I expect this awful rebellion would be over by now."

"You are sounding a lot like your father, Joshua," the minister declared. "Cyrus would be proud. Don't get any strange ideas like he's had about giving compensation to all *slaves* when they are freed, though." He smirked before turning back to Mr. Mullins.

"I don't know if I would be so quick to come around to John Woolman's way of thinking myself. I think we need the slaves and the slaves need us, though I certainly don't support secession. Lord knows, I'm a Unionist through and through. My son's even fighting for the Union right now."

To Joshua's relief, the subject changed. After spending the morning with Jim and Pete, he was in no mood for this.

It was Mr. Mullins who diplomatically shifted the focus of the conversation. "So, Rev. Johnson, please tell us more about the Shawnee Indian Mission School."

The minister pulled himself up so his huge frame sat even taller. "It's over in Kansas, a few miles from where we sit," he replied. "Just across the state line.... I was head of that school for twenty-eight years. My wife and I started it way back in 1830. Then, I turned it over to my son five years ago."

"Oh, yes—1830, the year of the Indian Removal Act," Grandpa Carter mused.

"Indeed it was, Mr. Carter," Rev. Johnson agreed. "The government had to do *something* to manage the Indian problem."

"Of course," Homer nodded, agreeably. "We can't let those savages keep getting in the way of progress."

Joshua, now sitting right next to Rev. Johnson, could hardly contain himself. Grandpa only revealed his Cherokee heritage when it was to his advantage. Slim chance it would be now. He glanced across the table at "Uncle Sam," as he sometimes lovingly referred to Mr. Mullins, who was working as hard as Joshua to keep a straight face.

Rev. Johnson was apparently clueless as to how everyone else felt—or maybe it just didn't matter.

Next, he shocked them with a story about Mrs. Johnson's family. "The Indians got upset over some little somethin', as they are prone to easily do. As a result, my mother-in-law, who was a teenager at the time, was captured by them and separated from her family for years. Guess they treated her well, though—at least that's what she reported when she returned to her family. She learned their language really well, too—in fact, that came in handy for my wife and me in our work. See, Sarah picked up the language from her mother, as a child. That helped her figure out really fast what the children at the Mission were saying to one another that they might not want us to know."

Homer Carter's ability to juggle honesty with empathy shined through remarkably at this point.

"It's too bad what happened to that young girl," he said with the utmost compassion. "Too bad so many white folks have failed to respect Indian landowners, too. Like when Tecumseh went on a rampage a while back. As I recall, it happened when he discovered white men had gotten some of his tribesmen drunk before obtaining their signatures on an agreement to give up vast portions of their land. I suppose Tecumseh shouldn't have been so upset about something small as that, though."

Rev. Johnson picked right up and started talking again. Seems he never noticed the sullen smiles of Sam and Joshua. "My wife and I did our best to see all the children boarding at our school were well cared for," he explained. "How I loved those children! I even hired a new female slave every year to be sure we had plenty of help. We wanted to teach them without the influence of their parents, of course. That was important. We trained them to make a living, tried hard to civilize them, too. Taught a lot of 'em to make a good living now, using our farming methods. The girls learned to cook and sew, boys did cabinetry and mechanics. I even used my store for their benefit, still do. I give them a fair price for what they make and then sell it in my store. We saw to it that they learned English very well, too—now that's progress!" he exclaimed, doubling his fist to strike the table for emphasis. "But no matter what we did, we couldn't seem to change them as much as we'd hoped. Leave 'em alone and most of 'em go right back to their same old ways of yore."

"We even taught my little slave children to read and write. It didn't matter to me if it was forbidden by law. Yet the government closed us down a year after the rebellion. They took the money the school needed and used it for the war instead. Unfortunately, there weren't many Indians wanting to send their children to us anymore by then. They went back to keeping them home and teaching them the way they always had. It's a shame. I just don't know what we're goin' to do in this country to manage the Indian problem."

"Guess all we can do is to keep destroying their way of life, stealing their land, and driving them toward the Pacific Ocean as far as they'll go," Homer scoffed.

About then, Rev. Johnson choked on a crumb of cornbread.

"Excuse me, Rev. Johnson. I'm not feeling well. Would you mind showing Joshua and me to our room?" Grandpa asked.

Soon the two were sound asleep, side by side, in the tall grass out back of the house, atop a patchwork quilt that Grandpa found across his bed. "I could never sleep a wink under the same roof with that scoundrel," he told Joshua.

To **learn more** about John Woolman's interesting approach to slavery you can listen to podcasts about him at:

http://www.woodbrooke.org.uk/pages/qsrc-podcasts.html

27

"When things start wrong, they stay wrong for a long, long time." Those words were the last thing he'd heard last night, looking at the stars from the same spot where he now lay. The boy gazed at a tiny, fluffy cloud that seemed to hold little promise of much-needed rain for the long day ahead.

Was Grandpa referring to slavery or what Rev. Johnson called "the Indian problem?" Could be either one, he decided—or both.

His father could make a whole month's study out of Grandpa's one line, no doubt taking his students back for centuries. He'd be sure to include the Constitution, how imperfect it was, how the founding fathers thought it was the best they could do on the slavery issue. Borrowing words from Grandpa, he'd go on to say that many of the native inhabitants of the soil being claimed by these newcomers already knew those men were "speaking with a forked tongue." In the Constitution, they never even used the word "slave." Yet it was obvious that it existed and would continue to exist from the way things were worded.

Yesterday, right before he and Mrs. Wornall walked out of the music room together, she'd told him, "Good piano students learn quickly how to make harmony. Otherwise, they just create dissonance instead of pleasant music."

Dissonance … the Founding Fathers agreed to keep the dissonance instead of working longer to create the "real music" called for by the Declaration of Independence. Now, after so many slaves had suffered the devastating consequences, this dissonance had become so maddening it was impossible for sane folks to ignore. At least, that's how Joshua saw it.

The annoying rooster was being interrupted now by the persistent cry of the mourning doves. Like old friends, the familiar softness of their cries soothed both his thoughts and frustrations.

Suddenly it dawned on him. The old red rooster was like the dissonance, the things that had started wrong and stayed wrong for a long, long time. The mourning doves were voices of hope in spite of the sorrow.

It was time to take on a new day.

As the Mullins family climbed in the wagon right after breakfast, they only spoke of the grand reunion ahead.

Lucy had other things to think about. She wanted to look her best for the trip to the District of the Border Headquarters that afternoon. If all went well, she could be back with her children by suppertime with news of their father. If she got bad news, they might all be grieving.

"So, let's go over some assignments for the day," she said as soon as the Mullins left. "Joshua, you have sole care of Baby George and Jenny. Billy, you'll have the day free once you tidy up our sleeping quarters. Tom, you're to stay out of trouble and listen to Grandpa. He's not feeling well, so all of you be good."

And with that, she was gone. Joshua nodded respectfully to his mother, but frowned as soon as he started walking toward the porch where his baby brother and little sister sat. Before he got to them, he was smiling—not because he felt like smiling—but in the hopes his cheerfulness might be contagious. If so, maybe these two wouldn't whine for their mama all morning. With no nannies around now, he was "Chief Big Brother," once again.

How would he ever get the chance to play Annie-Over with these two hanging on him all day? Maybe he could at least find time to visit with Solomon, a new friend he'd met at breakfast.

Thanks to Alice, the two boys had a chance for Annie-Over all morning. The cute girl with the dark brown pigtails volunteered to care for Jenny and Baby George. Yet he wasn't sure how much she was watching the little ones. Every time he looked her way, her hazel eyes were fixed on him.

"Thank you," he told her at noon as he approached the table she'd chosen. "I'll be glad to help feed these two."

It was all he could do to keep from laughing. Apparently, Alice thought a nine-month-old baby could manage soup on his own. Expertly, Joshua took the spoon from the screaming child, removed his soiled shirt, and used it to mop soup off the little mouth, hands, and belly. Soon the infant eagerly slurped large spoonfuls of the liquid and gave his big brother a toothless grin.

"Oh, so that's how you do it!" exclaimed Alice. She giggled and turned to assist Jenny. "I'm the youngest of ten children, don't know much about babies," she explained.

"So how many of you are still at home?" he asked.

"None of us!" exclaimed Alice. "Leaving anybody back home would be much too dangerous."

Again, Joshua tried not to laugh. "You're right, Alice," he agreed. "Of course, none of us know what to call home now. What I meant to ask is if you have other siblings here with you."

"Oh, I see," she returned. "My three sisters are here. My brothers are off fighting for the Confederacy except for one. Mama took him to ride with William Quantrill two years ago after Papa got killed by jayhawkers."

"So where are you from?" Joshua asked.

"The southern part of Bates County. Took us a week to get here," she replied. "We came by wagon train. Four other women and their children travelled with us. Mama thought it might be safer that way."

"So you all have horses?" Joshua asked.

"Not any good ones. The one our family has is mighty old and lame. Others got oxen or mules apullin' their load."

"I know all about traveling with a mule," Joshua said with a sigh, though he wouldn't have dared tell her of his recent adventures.

"The worst part wasn't the animals for us," Alice continued. "It was the mamas. Somehow they all managed to get along back home with the men gone. Out on the road, with all the tension, things changed. A Unionist started fighting with a Secessionist—I mean fighting to the point of hair-pulling. They're still not speaking, but my mama got the fight broke up. Now, the next problem will be finding separate places for all of us to go, cause there's no way we can live together in the same house. Good thing Rev. Johnson has agreed to help us. He says we can stay here as long as necessary. He's even gonna loan us money. What a godsend!"

Joshua decided it was time to change the subject.

"I better get these two a nap," he told her. "I'll come find you when they're up."

"Oh, certainly!" Alice said, a little more enthusiastic than necessary. I'll be in the girls' dormitory."

"Dormitory?"

"That's what Mrs. Johnson calls it. She cleared an extra-large bedroom for all us girls. There's a smaller room for Solomon and the younger boys in our traveling party."

"So you've known Solomon a long time, then?"

Alice grinned sheepishly. "We were sweethearts until this morning," she said.

Joshua gulped. Suddenly he understood why Solomon left the lunch table so quickly.

Billy studied the hand-made ball all morning long while playing Annie-Over. It was sewn from multiple layers of scraps cut from old wagon sheets. Mrs. Johnson patted him on the head as she handed him the cloth he'd requested and a big pair of scissors. He didn't ask for needle and thread—he got those out of Ma's knapsack. By two o'clock, he'd managed to stitch together a baseball that looked a lot like Frank's. Swelling with pride, he admired the creation.

There was only one problem. It needed more weight. So he tore the ball open, put a couple of rocks in the center, and stitched it all up again.

Meanwhile, Luke found a piece of wood for a bat. Billy whittled one end to make a handle. They were all set.

Soon, they had two teams organized. Billy thought the girls should just stick to batting while he pitched for both teams. They had a grand time, until the third inning, that is. That's when one of the girls hit a real slugger!

Seeing the blood spurting from her brother's head, Jenny was terrified.

"I wish I'd never seen a baseball," wailed Billy as Grandpa poured Lugol's solution all over the gash. As any boy knew, that stuff only added insult to the misery of any wound. Full of iodine, it burned like fire. Yet doctors and mothers alike swore by it.

The boy hardly moved until late afternoon. His head throbbed. Worse, he was humiliated—first from the accident, more so from Grandpa lecturing him about his foolish mistake of putting rocks in the middle of that homemade ball.

Of course, when he saw his mother step finally step from the wagon that evening, he expected some sympathy. Instead she needed comfort more than he did.

Rev. Miller escorted her to the big porch near their bedroom. Whatever she'd learned, anyone could tell it wasn't good.

"How are my babies?" she asked Joshua as he came out to greet her.

"They're fine, Ma," he said soothingly, "I've had plenty of help today."

Putting his arm around her shoulders, the two of them walked toward the porch, where Mrs. Johnson had just placed three chairs before politely excusing herself.

Rev. Miller was there, speaking in muffled tones. "Joshua, I'm sorry to tell you that we learned nothing more about your father."

Quickly gaining her composure, Lucy Carter took it from there. "He may be in prison, Joshua, as we suspected. That's probably the best hope we have. Nobody can say for sure, though. The Union can't keep up with all the prisoners, nor do they try."

Her words, interspersed with sobs, came slower and slower. "If your father .... is in prison, ... we don't even know which one. They don't even allow mail in and out of most military prisons!" she blurted out.

"What did General Ewing say?" Joshua asked his former minister, whose eyes were filling with tears, same as Joshua's.

"We never saw General Ewing," he replied. "He wasn't available. Instead we were taken right in to General Schofield. That's Ewing's boss. The man's not known for compassion or tact. So be gentle with your mother. It will take a while for her to recover."

In Joshua's opinion, his mother never recovered. Her going to Union headquarters seemed to be a big mistake. For more than a year, she would refuse to discuss it again.

At suppertime Lucy declared she wasn't hungry. Joshua was just about to say that he was when he heard Mr. Wornall talking.

"Eliza is worried, Homer. As soon as I told her about our conversation at headquarters, she insisted I come right over. She and Aunt Molly have everything set up for you to stay, and I have you three cabins booked for Saturday morning on one of the finest steamboats on the Missouri River.

28

Here we go again, Joshua thought. It wasn't that he didn't like the new plans--just with things changing constantly, they never knew what to count on. That was the hardest part about being needy. You had to depend on others to figure a lot of things out.

At least, the shopping plans were still on. He could hardly wait. From what Frank described yesterday, this store carried ready-made clothes—something he'd never owned in his life.

Quickly the family thanked the Johnsons and squeezed into the carriage with all their belongings. No time to even bid farewell to Alice or Solomon. Rev. Johnson and his wife didn't seem offended at their sudden departure. Perhaps they were glad to have space for the new family that had arrived an hour ago.

At least, the children knew what to count on again for the next few hours. Except from their mother, who was grumpier than they'd ever seen.

*****

"September's usually slow, that being the end of traveling

season," Rev. Johnson explained next morning as he pulled the carriage up to the front door of Johnson's Trading Post. "Most folks hit the Santa Fe Trail or leave for points west earlier in the summer. Thanks to the General Ewing, we got a new wave of travelers this year. They're desperate for what we got, and I'm doing my best to accommodate."

Tom's eyes were as big as saucers. His head made two rotations from Grandpa's face, to Billy's, to Joshua's, then back as he gazed at the storefront. He wasn't the only one in shock. This store was six times larger than the one at Hickman Mills.

Inside, multi-colored Indian blankets covered the walls. "Perfect for Iowa winters," Rev. Johnson declared, stacking a dozen of them on a table. Shirts of all sizes, suspended on twisted pieces of wire, brought to Joshua's mind the image of skeletons that haunted him daily.

Instantly, he turned to examine an array of gadgets on a glass-topped counter.

"This is just what you need, Joshua," Grandpa suggested, handing him an odd, black leather pouch. "The way things are going, I suspect it will come in mighty handy."

*****

Lucy could hardly contain her joy at seeing all the new shoes.

"Look what else I got," Tom said, rushing to show off his harmonica. "Billy got a baseball, too, and Joshua, an ammunition pouch."

Oh, oh! The six-year-old scampered. Seeing the shock on his mother's face, he wasn't sticking around to hear what came next.

"Just what are you teaching this child, Joshua Carter?" Lucy asked from the rocking chair where she was nursing Baby George. "The last thing I want any of you to have is ammunition."

"It was Grandpa's idea," Joshua explained meekly. He turned around, fully expecting to have help in explaining. To his surprise, they'd all deserted him—including Grandpa.

Staring at his mother's furrowed brow, he took a deep breath.

"I'm not lying, Ma," he said. "Grandpa says if I keep on, someday I'll have this pouch filled with ideas more powerful than anything that can be loaded into a gun."

She didn't move a muscle. Until he finally broke the silence neither did he.

"Don't you see, Ma?" He tilted his head. His eyes narrowed as he waited for an answer.

She only stared back blankly.

"You understand, don't you?" his pleading voice continued.

Her eyes brightened as ever-so-gradually the corners of her mouth rose. "Just be careful how you use your ammunition, son," she warned, her faint smile fading almost as soon as his began.

Upstairs, he found his grandfather. "I'm worried about Ma," he said.

"Oh, she'll be fine once she gets on that steamboat," Grandpa insisted. "Meanwhile, we gotta get these steamer trunks packed."

29

Had Cyrus Carter passed his family boarding the steamboat at Westport, he wouldn't have recognized them. The sombreros, one on each boy's head, were the most striking of all their new duds.

He definitely wouldn't have recognized Tom with blotches all over his face. The kid had cried since 3 a.m. when his mother, coming in to wake him, discovered a knife tucked under his pillow—fortunately in a sheath.

"I need that!" he screamed, seeing she was confiscating it. "Frank says I have to have it 'cause of all the pirates on the river."

No amount of reasoning could convince the boy he would have no use for the knife, on the river or anytime soon. "I'll keep it in a safe place for you until you're older," Ma promised before she packed it at the bottom of her *own* trunk and carefully hid the key.

Now, as they walked up the gangplank, the little pouter was missing all the fun, even ignoring the fascinating bells and musical whistles. He didn't crack a smile when Billy declared some of them sounded like Grandpa blowing his nose. "Be careful, Tom," his mother warned. "If you put your bottom lip out any further, somebody may step on it." At that, the kid's eyes only narrowed more.

"Just for good measure, let me go over the warnings one more time," Mr. Wornall said. "Stay up on the second deck, where your cabins are located. Most passengers stay on first deck to save money. It's filthy and crowded on first deck with all the animals and cargo. You can't close your eyes a minute for fear of getting robbed, kicked, or spat on by some scoundrel, if not the deck hands themselves. Lots of fights on first deck."

Joshua wished the warnings would cease. His nervous mother was already anxious enough. Besides, he'd memorized it all the first time.

"You'll have fine dining and cabin crew to assist you with your baggage. Guard you belongings. Never know who might be up to mischief. With so many bushwhackers gone south, you shouldn't run into many of them, though. Whatever you do, the children must not climb on the railing. Keep them away from the saloon doors, boys—too much gambling and fighting going on there." All of this rang in Joshua's ears as he helped put their things in their cabins and rushed out on the upper deck to watch the crew load cargo and animals while lower deck passengers waited, hoping to find room to stretch their legs a little.

Everything is in order, Joshua told himself. Then, he smiled, thinking how different it was being ordered to do something as opposed to having friends setting things in motion to ease their way. He felt truly blessed.

*****

As they sat in the dining room, feasting on a luxurious lunch of roasted lamb, Lucy Carter asked Joshua about the papers Mr. Wornall handed him just before they boarded. "Have you taken time to look at them yet?" she wondered.

"No, but I have them right here," Joshua answered, giving his pouch a couple of pats. "It's an article from an issue of *Harper's Weekly* last month. Mr. Wornall said it would show there are a lot more people like Pa than any of us have realized. Here, you can read it for yourself, Ma."

Billy and Joshua sat quietly, gazing out at the water through the dining room windows, as they leisurely cruised up the Missouri. It was several minutes before their mother handed the papers back to Joshua.

"You can explain it all to Billy when you've finished reading it," she told him. "It's interesting, I must say.....a bit comforting, too."

Mark, their German cabin attendant, had been working up and down the Missouri for five years.

"Been all the way to Montana," he declared before showing them around. "As long as the captain steers clear of sandbars and felled tree below the water's surface, we do just fine. Indians are the only other problem. They don't think kindly about steamboats, but you don't need to worry in this neck of the woods."

He pointed to a door just past Lucy's room. "The toilet is here, right over the paddle wheel," he informed them. "You'll find a comb and brush lying near the washbowl. You are welcome to use them, same as everybody else."

"Yes, thanks," returned Joshua. "I saw those already, but there's another object I don't recognize."

"It's this thing," Joshua said, as he rushed in and back out, holding up a skinny brush with a long handle.

"Oh!" Mark's eyes brightened. "It's a toothbrush. Lots of our passengers have never seen one. I'll show you how to use it." After the expert demonstration, followed by a quick rinse, he handed the brush back to his young guest.

"My teeth never felt so clean!" Joshua exclaimed minutes later. "Back home, we just use a small green twig and a little baking soda every Saturday along with our baths. Maybe I can talk Ma into getting one of these for our family soon."

30

"Pirates! I knew I'd need that knife!" Tom shouted. At that, his big brothers, both napping nearby, shot straight up.

Joshua's heart pounded as he darted out the door. There must have been a dozen gunshots already and no sign of them stopping. Where was that boy? Which way did he go? Taking a guess, he dashed back to the stairs that descended near the paddle wheel.

Relieved to find the six-year-old standing still at the foot of the stairs, he cautiously stopped four steps above. The shooting had ceased, but what was Tom staring at? From the color of his face, it could easily be a dead man or maybe several.

Joshua was more confused as he took his place beside the child, still standing like a statue. Nobody else seemed upset. In fact, they were quite amused. Had Tom seen something that nobody else did?

"They were just having fun," a nicely-dressed lady offered, turning her attention their way. "No harm done. Shooting at wildlife from steamboats is a common sport."

"Why would they shoot at something they can't even eat?" asked Joshua, genuinely puzzled.

Nobody answered, nor seemed to even hear.

Tom, still staring at the same spot, was transfixed.

"Did you see the animals they were aiming at?" Joshua asked, kneeling and gently touching Tom's shoulder.

Tom slowly shook his head from side to side. "No. I would love to have seen the animals, but they got scared off. The only one I see now is the little deer they killed," he said sadly. "See it over by that tree?"

The trees were hardly visible now, but it didn't matter. More important was Tom's wounded heart. It was all so senseless.

"That sort of tomfoolery is one reason most Indians don't like steamboats," Mark said moments later. Out of concern, he'd come searching for the boys.

Back upstairs, Grandpa walked out on deck looking bleary-eyed.

"You didn't sleep through all that, did you?" Joshua asked.

"All what?" the old man replied.

Joshua rolled his eyes. "Grandpa, if you have to ask what, you were definitely asleep," he said.

Lucy's experience had been just the opposite. She craned

her neck out around the door to survey the faces of the others. "Would somebody please tell me what those shots were all about? I've been afraid to come out."

Mark saved Joshua the trouble of explaining. "Everything is fine, Mrs. Carter, a rather routine occurrence here on the Missouri. If you care to join me in the dining room, I'll tell you all about it. Meanwhile, I'd be happy to hold this big boy for you. He reminds me of my own son."

Baby George leaped into Mark's outstretched hands as if he'd known the man all his life.

Ma's question about the gunfire was soon forgotten, replaced by a question from Billy. "How old is this boat?" he called from the back of the line.

"Just two years old," Mark yelled back. "Most boats on this brutal river don't last more than five." He motioned toward a table, pulling a chair out for Lucy, before putting the baby back in her arms. "Didn't I hear someone say that you'll also be going up the Mississippi in a few days?" he asked.

Lucy nodded.

"Well, the Mississippi is wider, more predictable and a lot easier to navigate. So those boats last a lot longer." he explained.

"So tell us about *your* family? Where do they stay while you travel?" Lucy asked.

"Our home is here in St. Joe," he replied. "Me and the missus got three little ones and are also raising my little brother and sister. My parents died two years back of cholera in the same week. On account of that, I got an exemption from military service to take care of the two orphans. So here I am doing my duty to my country, making a living on the river."

"Seems life's not easy for anybody these days," muttered Joshua.

The attendant went to the kitchen and came back with a tray

of cool water and a pot of coffee.

"I'm tryin' to decide if I should go north again this year. It's more dangerous, but the pay's much better up there, though it's not bad anywhere due to the shortage of experienced men these days."

"Do you have a favorite captain?" Homer asked.

"Oh, yes sir! Captain La Barge. He was called into service by the Union earlier this year, making trip after trip to get supplies down to Vicksburg. Used the best and finest boat around, one he built with his own hands, called her *Emilie*. Oh, how he loved that boat!

"Well, I tell you what's right--the Union has a way of deciding what they want and getting it. It didn't quite work out that way with Captain La Barge, though. The Union told him he couldn't take his *Emilie* back north again 'cause the army needed it. So right away he up and sold her to the railroad and caught a ride with his brother, going north on another boat. Never have found out if the railroad ended up with *Emilie* or the Union got her.

"If I was to go north, I'd want to go with Captain La Barge. He had an awful encounter with the Sioux this summer, though. From what I hear, things went sour because one of those crooked Indian agents tried to cheat the Sioux. Wasn't the captain's fault. He was just trying to do his job. Some of the Sioux thought they could destroy the steamboat by putting out the fires in the engine. Of course, that didn't destroy the boat, but it definitely got it stopped for a while. In the end several crew members and a lot of Sioux ended up dead."

"So you say the Sioux don't like the steamboats?" said Joshua.

"No, not one bit! Besides the wildlife, they say the boats are destroying their land. They don't like the noise either," replied Mark. But things are changing since some of the Indians are using boats for trading purposes. They love the little trinkets and novelties the white men have, so they bring furs, vegetables, and their own handiwork in exchange. Of course, with them not knowing the value of some of the items, the white men tend to make great profits at the expense of the red man."

"Yes, if the white men all had good, honest intentions, we could all live peaceably together," Homer spoke up.

"Sadly, government agents are provoking the Sioux an awful lot these days, too," noted the attendant.

Billy was curious. "So what do the Sioux want agents to do differently?"

"Simply honor the treaties, which call for the Indians to receive specific amounts of money for the use of their land. Some agents put the money in their own pockets, and the Indians never see it. Things have gotten worse since the Great Rebellion started because the Union has the agents telling the Indians that their money must now go to war effort."

"I bet the Indians don't take kindly to that," declared Grandpa.

"They certainly don't." Mark agreed. "The Sioux are asking why the soldiers get paid while they have to wait."

"It's a fair question, I'd say," Ma said.

"Did I hear you say that the steamboat industry is thriving in Montana?" Joshua asked.

"Oh, yes. Lots of deposits have been discovered there just this year. They have entire communities popping up with the funniest names. Alders Gulch and Grasshopper Creek, for instance—on account of the plague of grasshoppers folks had to fight on top of the crowds crawling all over one another to get to the gold."

They were all laughing as they visualized the scene.

"So the great flux of miners must be helping the steamboat industry a lot," Grandpa surmised.

"It's that and the new trail through Montana, going all the way to Oregon. It's easier than any of the other trails west. So they're packing people along with lots of cargo. Some stop to mine gold, then take their riches right on to the west coast. With all the demand, steamboat fares are extravagant. I tell you, business couldn't be better."

The loud whistle overhead had everyone's full attention.

"I do hope you've enjoyed your time on *Prosperity*," Mark said as he hurried to clear the table.

Joshua was puzzled until he stepped off the gangplank and looked back at the ship. Since they'd boarded before daylight, he'd not noticed the big letters on the side of the boat until now. So that's what Mark meant. "Prosperity" was the steamboat's name, perfect after what they'd just learned about her.

Quickly, Mark hailed a wagon and helped the driver hoist the steamer trunks into it. "There's a fine hotel between here and my house if I can ride along and give you a hand," he offered.

"Oh, that would be wonderful!" Lucy exclaimed. They all climbed onto the two seats lining the sides of the wagon bed and soon found themselves approaching a building at least twice the size of Prosperity.

"Patee House," Joshua said, reading the sign. "Is this a hotel? Can we stay here?"

"The Patee House is almost brand new and one of the best hotels in the whole nation, but I'm sure you don't want to be their guest right now," Mark said with one raised eyebrow. "Most ordinary folks who get in this building are taken directly to the big, fine ballroom upstairs. Not for a ball, though. They've made it into a courtroom, from which many men go straight to the gallows.

"The Union army took it over and hauled Mr. Patee, the unfortunate owner, off to prison for being disloyal. Thanks to his friends, he got released. Yet he can't do a thing but wait to see what will be left of his fine establishment once the Union is finished with it."

Mark found them a fine hotel nearby and wished them well as he thanked Lucy for the nice tip and turned to go home. If he happened to notice the sobering effect his remarks brought on his listeners, he never let on. Just as well he knew nothing about Pa, Joshua thought. Mark had troubles of his own.

31

Lucy Carter seemed deep in thought—actually deep in despair, thought Joshua.

"Just bring me something to eat if you want," she said, not wanting to leave the hotel when everyone went out to explore the town Sunday afternoon.

"Until Ma met with General Schofield, our worries were mostly about Pa. Now, we've got her to worry about, too," Joshua said, jostling Baby George in his arms.

"She'll be okay, once she gets on the train tomorrow," Grandpa told him as he looked across the street where the other three children were playing near the Pony Express office.

"That's what you said about her getting on the steamboat," Joshua countered.

"She just needs to stay busy, keep her mind occupied. You'll see. Got an idea...." Next, with a glint in his eye, Grandpa leaned across the table and whispered. "Mr. Wornall put some money in my pocket yesterday morning." He dug deep into his trousers and pulled out a dollar bill. "Betcha somewhere around here we can find a set of checkers."

"That will perk her up," Joshua agreed. "She loves checkers."

They found the checkers, all right—but, in the meantime, they totally forgot about the younger kids. When they caught up with them, the three were pestering a woman selling vegetables outside the Pony Express office. Billy was interested in getting a job. Tom wanted to know if the next rider might take them for a ride around St. Joe in his spare time. And Jenny just watched as the perturbed lady tried to explain that no riders would be coming."

"Why not?" Tom moaned.

"Hm-m-m," grunted the woman. "That would take the rest of the day to explain … Pony Express had trouble from the day it started. Would have been nice if it'd worked …didn't even last two years between corrupt management and Indian attacks … folded right up soon as The War for Independence began."

They gave up on finding a checker board, but this wasn't stopping Joshua. Back in the hotel, he pulled out two sheets of clean paper, used *Uncle Tom's Cabin* for a straight edge, and soon had a fine board drawn off.

The sandwich and a checker tournament did the trick for Lucy Carter. She forgot all her worries about getting on the train until the next morning.

*****

"Don't you worry, ma'am," the ticket master assured her. "There will be soldiers stationed at every bridge. It's the bridges where we're most likely to run into trouble with the Confederates. We haven't had any big problems in months, though. You can just sit back and relax."

"How long will the trip take?" Grandpa asked.

"It's hard to say," replied the porter, lifting their trunks onto the baggage car. "Depends on how long we have to spend at each of the twenty-three stops. Used to, the trip took twelve hours. Whole purpose, originally, was to provide fast, convenient transportation for private citizens. Nowadays what the Union needs gets priority, so we're weighted down with lots of freight. Plus, with all the soldiers goin' an' comin,' it takes a lot of time to load and offload."

Joshua started off counting the stops, thinking it would help pass the time. As it turned out, he got so occupied with other things that he abandoned his efforts midway through the trip.

What fun it was trying to spot partially-concealed troops guarding the tracks! Easy, too, with the advantage their elevated view provided.

By the fourth stop, Jenny was whining. Ma passed around some berries she'd bought at the train station. Joshua moved over and sat next to Billy at stop number fourteen. By then, they were the only two awake.

"What about those papers you're supposed to explain to me?" Billy asked.

Joshua removed a clipping from his pouch and handed it to his brother. "Back in July, there were riots in New York City," he explained. "They were incited by people upset because of the draft that Pa chose to ignore. People up there say it's not fair to the poor."

"How come?" Billy asked as he glanced at the article.

"Because anyone with three-hundred dollars to spare can pay to have somebody fight in their place," Joshua replied. "Over a hundred people got killed in these riots, Billy. It was mostly Negroes. See, the majority of the rioters were poor Irishmen, blaming the war on Negroes."

"That's not fair!" exclaimed Billy.

Joshua shrugged. "No, it's not. Lots of things aren't fair these days. President Lincoln tried to stop the uprising, but troops couldn't get there fast enough. So the rioters destroyed big buildings and churches, too.

Next thing out of the pouch was a page from *Harper's Weekly*. "This was in Pa's tin," Joshua continued. "Seems he thought a lot about this man named Elihu Burritt who proposed a plan for avoiding this whole war. Some believe he presented it to Abraham Lincoln even before he was elected President."

"I think I heard Pa and Ma talking about that in the night one time a while back," Billy said, "didn't understand it all, though."

"Well, it would have set slaves free, but it would have also helped the masters. Burritt called for the government to purchase the slaves from their masters, find jobs for them, and set them free. He even wrote a book about his ideas for peace, entitled *Citizen of the World*. See?" Joshua said, pointing to the title in the article.

"So wouldn't President Lincoln have read that book?"

"No doubt he did. I think Pa would have gotten along well with Burritt if the two could have met. Guess he got tired of people in Washington not listening to his ideas, though. He took off to England, where he's finding people more receptive."

"Do you suppose anybody else in Missouri agreed with Burritt?" Billy asked.

"Not that I know of, but 50,000 in the North signed up to join the movement years before the Great Rebellion." Joshua explained. "They even had a convention in 1856 to promote compensated emancipation. Rev. Johnson made fun of the whole idea during a discussion we had after you went off to bed at his place."

"So why do you think so many refused to listen to Burritt?" Billy asked.

"I think there are too many stubborn people on both sides, who cared about having their way rather than working for peace ... still are," Joshua replied. "Another thing I saw in Pa's notes: he believed what an editor named Garrison said, that if the people in the North would stop buying products made by slaves, slavery would not long survive. Seems to me Burritt would like that idea, too."

"I wish Pa could meet Elihu Burritt," Billy said, wistfully.

"Maybe he can someday," Joshua asserted.

Suddenly, without warning, they were almost jolted out of their seats as the train slowed down abruptly. What was that? Seconds later they picked up speed again. The two brothers looked at one another and shrugged.

"What did we hit?" a soldier in blue asked the conductor, who'd just come from the front of the train.

"Just a flock of sheep—seems no serious harm was done," the conductor replied. "We'll see when we get to the next station."

"No serious harm to the sheep or to the train?" asked the soldier. His friends enjoyed a hearty laugh.

"What stop is next?" Joshua asked the conductor.

"Brookfield," the man said. "We'll have time for all of you to stretch your legs there. Brookfield usually has ladies with good, hot lunches and pies ready to sell"

At least a dozen ladies were waiting as promised. While Grandpa and Billy bought lunch for everyone, Joshua followed Jenny around outside the station.

"Look, Joshua!" she suddenly cried, yanking hard on her big brother's hand.

"If that don't beat all," the conductor, kneeling beside Tom, was saying. In his arms, he held a tiny lamb.

With Joshua and his sister now approaching, the man looked at Jenny and smiled. "This little fellow got a breezy ride after the rest of the sheep were killed. He was up front, caught in the grill, but he's safe and sound now."

"He's shaking!" cried Jenny.

"What will become of him without his mother?" Tom asked, tears glistening in his eyes.

"We'll let him stay right here at the station. He'll make a good pet," another man, wearing a striped hat, said as he gently carried the animal inside.

No harm done? Joshua posed the question to himself while he gently boosted his little sister up and across the steep steps of the train again.

After a hearty lunch, he took the two pieces of paper he'd stuffed in his pouch that morning. He had a lot to write about progress before they got to their day's final destination.

*****

"This is Hannibal," several passengers announced in unison long after dark.

Joshua closed *Uncle Tom's Cabin*. He was glad for a break in the reading. The part he'd just finished left him with a heavy heart. In the story, Uncle Tom was beside the slave trader. They were traveling south, further and further from Uncle Tom's family. Barring some miracle, he'd never see them again.

To **learn more** about the Enrollment Act of 1863 and why the draft was considered by protestors to be unfair, visit:

http://www.yale.edu/glc/archive/962.htm

32

"The moment I pulled aside that lovely, calico curtain, something washed over my soul," Lucy said for years to come. *"My whole head was as clear as the sparkling water and my spirits soared like the gulls circling the charming steamboats, resting just two hundred feet from where I stood."*

"What a spectacular view! Come see, Joshua. We have four whole days to just explore this wonderful city," Ma beckoned to him in a whisper.

Suddenly he was wide awake. Ma hadn't sounded this excited since three years ago at Christmas. What had come over her?

"We made it to 'The Mighty Mississippi' and it's bigger than I ever imagined. Just look at the color!" she continued.

Carefully, Joshua tiptoed around the pallets of his younger siblings. "The boats look like floating castles!" Joshua gasped.

"Yes, and right now this room seems a bit like a castle. It's simple, but all we need."

A few trees on the far shore had started to turn, adding rusty red and golden glows to the soft blue trim of the white steamboats that rested lazily on the still water. Dark-skinned men lugging heavy cargo, scurried back and forth from the boats to stacks of wood and more freight on shore.

Joshua thought of the ant beds back home. As a small child, he'd watched for hours in admiration, fascinated as the industrious, little workers tirelessly carried loads much bigger than their tiny bodies. They always seemed to move under orders, with some kind of deadline—just like these men must be doing. The comparison left him with a strange mixture of sadness and curiosity. Something just wasn't right. Who were these men? What were they loading? How long had they worked like this? Did they have families? Where did they live?

Like his mother, he couldn't wait to get outside. He would relish the fresh air, same as she. Yet what intrigued him most, wherever he went, were the people.

*****

"How do you do it?" he asked Hector Collins, who, at fifteen, was the youngest son of the lady operating the boarding house. They'd spent the first hour of the morning at the dock, with Joshua mostly listening to conversations between Hector and the busy workers.

His new friend was puzzled. "How do I do *what*?" he asked.

"How do you get all these men to stop and talk to you? Why, you know them all by name!" exclaimed Joshua.

"Easy." Hector shrugged. "Many of them have known me all my life. My father *owns* that loading dock."

"Oh, I see. So they are workers, not slaves?" Joshua asked.

Hector shrugged again. "*Some* are slaves, others free. None belong to my father, though."

Joshua was confused.

"Pa's never owned slaves," Hector explained, "but he's a businessman who needs a lot of help. Here in Hannibal many slave masters hire their slaves out, so they get most of the earnings. They give their slaves a place to live and a little spending money from the deal. From what the men tell me, Pa is a lot kinder to them than most of their slave masters. They like working for him. He also sees they get their money instead of giving it directly to the slave masters like some others do. He knows the slaves may get cheated more than ever with that arrangement. So they trust him, and I guess that's why they trust me, too."

Downtown wasn't far away. It was bustling, with dozens of horses tethered near the stores. Hector pointed across the street to a building as large as Johnson's Trading Post. "Most days I'm in there working for my father. Not today, on account of you being here, but tomorrow morning I'll be back running errands, helping with payroll for the dock workers, then giving my mother a hand at the boarding house."

"Do you go to school?" Joshua inquired.

"Sometimes I do." said Hector, shrugging once again. "Don't know why I need to, though. I'm getting my education without a lot of book learning, between all the work, our visitors from near and far, and the steamboat workers who bring interesting news and stories almost every day. One of these days, I hope to be sitting in the pilot house of a boat like that one," he said, pointing to a craft with three decks.

"Grandpa thinks the railroad may put steamboats out of business in a few years," said Joshua as they turned back toward town, taking a left at the first corner.

"I can't imagine that!" exclaimed Hector. "I already seen how long it took just to get track laid from Hannibal to St. Joe." He pointed down the street. "It all started there in 1846, in the office of John Marshall Clemens, one of our attorneys. My oldest brother Eli was best friends with his son, Samuel. On that very day, the two sat on that porch shootin' marbles when a half dozen men walked out saying how they'd just started the first railroad west of the Mississippi. Well, Mr. Clemens died before they laid the first track, I'm sorry to say… Sam and Eli together made several trips on it since it was finished in 1859, though…. Good thing they got it done 'fore the war. Otherwise, it would be stopped halfway across the state, like the Burlington is in Iowa."

"The Burlington?" said Joshua. "That's the train we'll be taking to our new home."

"Guess they'll get the rest of that track laid, too, if ever we finish with this old war."

"We will," Joshua assured him. "I just wish it would be soon."

"Your pa? Where is he?" Hector asked.

Joshua chose his words carefully. "He's missing....took off to help after the massacre at Lawrence....never made it back home. We had to leave without him 'cause of Order No. 11."

"I know. I heard your mother talking this morning," Hector acknowledged. "Sorry about your Pa. My brother Will is missing, too. He went to fight for the rebels.... Eli is in Virginia somewhere, fighting for the Union. His wife and kids are at the boarding house."

He pointed across the street. "If Eli ever gets back, he wants to work at the newspaper office like Samuel Clemens once did." Conversation lulled as they turned again toward the river. "I think, with everything so uncertain, maybe we should all think about following Sam's example," Hector said. "He's already had four careers, and he's only twenty-eight."

"Four careers--what did he do besides work at the newspaper office?" Joshua asked.

"Well, it's quite a story," replied Hector. "For a little while, he was an artist....just made drawings for newspapers..... got one published in *Saturday Evening Post* before he turned seventeen. Guess he got bored with all of that, though. So he started working on steamboats when he was twenty-one— something he'd been dreaming of doing since he was a little kid. Even got his pilot's license four years ago, allowing him to sit on top instead of doing all the hard work below. He might still be doing that if it weren't for the war."

"So he's a soldier now," Joshua theorized.

"Oh, no," Hector replied. "Samuel's big brother got appointed by President Lincoln as Secretary of Nevada Territory, so he went along to help. Must not have helped too long, though. Next thing you know, he was into prospecting. Maybe he didn't have any luck finding gold or maybe he just got bored, didn't say ... but last year we got a letter from him, saying he's back in the newspaper business in Virginia City, Nevada."

"Virginia City?" Joshua was puzzled. "I heard about Virginia City from our cabin attendant on the steamboat we took to St. Joe. He said it was in Montana, though."

"Maybe there are two Virginia City's" suggested Hector. "All I know is Clement's letter was from Nevada."

Joshua shrugged and moved on. "The attendant also told us about a steamboat called *Emilie*," he said. "According to him, the owner sold it to a railroad this year when the Union wouldn't let La Barge take it back to Montana for his own business. Do you know anything about that?"

"Of course, I do. I know *all* about it," Hector answered. "It was the Hannibal-St. Joseph Railroad he sold it to for only $25,000. Right away, before the Union caught up with him, he took off to join his brother on another boat bound for Ft. Benton, Montana, where they got big business in gold and fur trading.

"I don't know what happened to the *Emilie*, but I can tell you Captain Joseph La Barge is one of the finest captains in the business. In fact, Samuel Clemens said it was from Captain La Barge he learned everything he needed to know about the craft."

"Wait a minute!" Joshua cried. "The way those two get around, maybe Samuel Clemens will find his way from Nevada up to Montana and return on one of La Barge's steamboats."

"Never can tell," agreed Hector.

33

Wednesday the two boys climbed to one of Hector's favorite lookouts. From there, they peered down over the smokestacks of colorful boats coming and going all afternoon.

It didn't take long for Joshua to realize how foolish his decision had been to leave the ammunition pouch behind. Yet he'd done so, fearful that Hector might think it silly.

He patted his shirt pocket. Not even a pencil and paper there.

The steamboats all had interesting names. He wanted to remember each one, but soon concluded it would be impossible to memorize them all. So he picked out a few and managed to get a rhythmical chant going in his mind. "*Halley's Comet, Sweet Swan, Garden City, Memphis Queen, Sultana*," he said, making up a little tune to go with it.

Sultana stuck in his head more than any other. Though an odd name, he could quickly associate it with the extremely *sultry* weather.

When he complained of the heat, Hector shrugged. "It's like this all summer here…on account of the humidity we get, being so close to the water."

Years later, Joshua would remember Hector's fond talk about the Sultana, how it was one of the best friends the North had, bringing such a steady stream of men and supplies down river. Of course, neither boy could imagine the tragic ending this ship would meet, taking 2300 newly-released prisoners down into a fiery, watery death at the close of the war. The explosion would lock the name Sultana in Joshua's mind, always taking him back to this carefree moment when he sat in wonder with his new friend.

"Do you have a favorite?" he asked Hector.

"Indeed I do! The boat my brother worked on. In fact, your family should take it. It comes to Hannibal on Thursday, leaves Friday. Isn't Friday when you plan to go?"

"Yes, it is. What's the boat's name?"

"*Sweet Betsy from Pike*," Hector replied, letting the words roll slowly off his lips.

"Where did they get a name like that?" Joshua asked, as he

tried tucking it into his chant.

"From a silly song about a woman named Betsy. Not a real woman, as far as I know. Guess she was from Pike County, just south of here, trying to get to California. The boat's owner hails from Pike County himself, I suppose he latched onto the name soon as he heard the song."

"Have you been on the boat?"

"Oh, yes! ….and I'm sure the captain will let me on to help you load."

*****

On Friday, Tom was the first guest at the breakfast table. There he sat, quietly wishing for another tall stack of pancakes like he'd had the day before."

"Good morning, Tom," Mrs. Collins called from the kitchen. "I've got enough hasty pudding for everyone to have two bowls full. Are you hungry?"

"Oh, yes, ma'am," the lad called back. "I'd love some hasty pudding!"

Truth is, as far as he knew, he'd never *tasted* it, though he frequently dreamed of doing so.

"Are you singing *again*?" Billy wasn't asking a question. He was complaining as he walked in with Joshua.

Ignoring the remark, Tom just kept repeating the second verse of "Yankee Doodle," always doubling back and starting over each time he got to the words "quick as hasty pudding."

"Everyone else must be sleeping in," Mrs. Collins said. At the other end of the table, Tom could see the steam rising from a half dozen bowls that rested on the large tray she carried.

If the cook noticed his displeasure when she sat his bowl in front of him, she didn't say a thing; but she couldn't ignore the look of disgust on his little face after the first bite.

155

"I'm sorry, lad," she said. "Is the hasty pudding not so tasty?"

"It's tasty enough," he politely replied, in a voice that failed to disguise his disappointment. "It's exactly like the porridge my mother makes. We just call it gruel."

About then, Mr. Collins entered, talking to Grandpa. "Every person who visits Hannibal simply *must* go to The Mississippi Express. It's a wonderful shop....used to be called Hannibal General Store. Soon as Maude Smith's husband went off to war, she hung a new sign out. Immediately, people started flocking to see if she'd changed anything besides the name. All she added were treats and a few tables, but business is booming now."

"Guess her husband will be surprised when he gets home."

"Like a lot of men will," Mr. Collins agreed. "With this war going on, women have a chance to show what they're made of. I expect men will be happy with some changes, unhappy with others." He paused to sip his coffee. "When you go, be sure to get a plate of Mrs. Smith's cry babies. The children will love them. I think they're quite good myself."

"We got enough cry babies at our house already," Billy chimed in.

Tom joined the roaring laughter, thankful the joke wasn't on him....or at least he didn't *know* it was on him.

The cry babies turned out to be molasses cookies. Mrs. Smith brought out a plate full. Baby George ate more than anyone, after which he promptly fell asleep beside Joshua.

Grandpa, still hungry, couldn't resist asking for "idiot's delight," the first item on the menu. As soon as Tom saw the vanilla custard, full of raisins and cinnamon, he talked his grandpa out of half a bowlful. It came much closer to meeting his expectations of hasty pudding.

Lucy wasn't interested in eating anything. What caught her

eye was the gold jewelry. Seeing her beam from ear to ear, Joshua decided it must be a sign something was coming alive again inside her. She'd never owned a piece of jewelry in her life.

Sitting on the end of a bench, he kept one hand on his sleeping baby brother while listening to the lively conversation from a nearby table.

"Some of my neighbors say there's a bill before Congress that would allow us in border states to sell our slaves to the Union," a man with his back against the wall was saying.

"What! Are you sure? That seems strange," the fellow across from him returned.

"It's a fact. That's how bad the Union needs soldiers. With so many casualties and desertions, they're desperate. I like the idea. This way niggers don't have to run off to join up like so many been doin'. Besides, I'd stand to get $1800 for my six men."

"So what would you do with the families?" asked the man across the table, rising to leave.

"Guess that's up to me....think they could go live at a military station....be considered contraband. You know, like property ... with protection, long as they behave themselves. So I would be shut of them all if I wanted to be."

Watching from the corner of his eye, Joshua could see the slave master had high hopes. How hard would it be for the men at the docks to choose between slavery and going into battle with the assurance of freedom afterwards? At least, they wouldn't have to worry about their wives and children being sold off somewhere else. If they agreed to fight, would they get paid? If so, would their pay be as much as that of white soldiers? What would their families have to go through at the military stations?

"If this keeps on, those abolitionists will have our kids *going to school* with niggers," said the fellow asking questions.

"Heck, if it keeps on, someday one of them niggers might even be President. Now, wouldn't that be somethin'?" the greedy slave master jeered as they walked out.

That night Joshua showed Hector everything--his pouch, the tin box of his father's, and his copy of *Uncle Tom's Cabin*. They talked far into the night.

"Have you thought about what you want to do with your life?" Hector asked.

Joshua surprised himself with his own answer. "I want to teach like my father." He stopped and looked out at the starry sky. "Or maybe publish a newspaper like Samuel Clemens," he added.

"Why not both?" his good buddy asked.

Perfect, thought Joshua, smiling through tightly pressed lips, but he said not a word.

Take a break and learn to make cry baby cookies! The recipe is at:

http://www.cooks.com/recipe/xm0bx6k0/cry-baby-cookies.html

34

The song "Sweet Betsy from Pike" was just three years older than the elegant steamboat. Inspired by the gold rush and written in 1858, it told the story of a couple, Betsy and Ike, going from Missouri to California, just as Hector said. With so much to see, the party atmosphere mesmerized even the adults.

Their attention was drawn to the Texas deck, where four men played an odd array of instruments outside the pilot house at the very top of the boat. Even from the distance, Tom recognized the distinct sound of the harmonica. Lucy knew the fiddle from a barn dance years ago. But the banjo was new to them all, and so was the washtub bass, the most fascinating of the four.

At the center of attention, a young Negro woman sang the complicated lyrics about "sweet Betsy" with confidence. Her voice was loud and clear above the talented instrumentalists.

"It sounds like she has a megaphone," Hector said, interrupting the trance that had come over each of the Carters. "It's the water.......music is always louder over water."

"Is that a fact?" Homer Carter returned, though Joshua noticed his grandfather was much more interested in the music. So was Joshua. If Tom planned to memorize all those lines, he had a lot of work ahead.

"Does the singer work on this boat regularly?" Lucy asked.

"Yes. Her name is Esther. She might be your chambermaid … also helps serve tea in the afternoons. The other musicians work in the kitchen or cabins. She's probably sang the entire song a dozen times already this morning. She does that over and over until everyone is on board. I think she's coming to the 5th verse." He stopped so they could all listen.

The wagon broke down with a terrible crash,

And out on the prairie rolled all sorts of trash.

"Sounds like what happened with the cart a few days ago." Billy's remark had everyone laughing.

It was the 13th verse, however, that changed Ma's mood instantly. "My children don't need to hear this," she complained to nobody in particular. Dashing off to the cabins on the upper deck only served to distract the younger children from catching the words. Joshua was quite amused as he listened to the 14th verse, which was even worse than the preceding one.

This Pike County couple got married, of course,

But Ike became jealous, and obtained a divorce.

Betsy, well-satisfied, said with a shout,

"Goodbye, you big lummox, I'm glad you backed out!"

"Scandalous, Hector! Absolutely scandalous!" roared Joshua, as the two set the largest steamer trunk near his bunk and plopped down, their sides splitting with laughter.

"Be sure to write, Joshua," Hector said, once he could resume talking. "I do hope we meet again." Of course, neither expected to nor could they predict the trouble that lay ahead for "Sweet Betsy from Pike".......the steamboat, that is. It's anybody's guess what happened to Betsy and Ike.

Esther noticed the clouds rolling in before any of the guests drinking their mid-afternoon tea. She had a habit of watching for ominous weather, as much as for ominous people. It was a useful habit for any woman working on the steamboats, considering all the characters as likely to show up as the unexpected thunderstorm. On the Mississippi, storms took out more boats than sandbars.

"Are we already to Keokuk?" Homer Carter asked Esther as she jumped from the sound of a thunderbolt while managing not to spill a drop of the steaming tea she was pouring.

"Yes, it's Keokuk, known as "Iowa's gate city." For the steamboat industry, this is a welcome site for crew bringing wounded or dying soldiers. Keokuk has five military hospitals," Esther explained. "For a city of just 13,000 people, that's a lot of hospitals. Sometimes after a big battle they'll bring two boatloads here at once. It's just an awful site to see those poor fellows."

"13,000 people in one city!" Joshua exclaimed from across the table. For any boy raised in Jackson County, this would be hard to imagine.

Esther laughed. "Yes, Keokuk's a lot bigger than Hannibal, but a dwarf compared to St. Louis, where I come from."

Strong flashes of lightning had their full attention. Joshua was fascinated, seeing how it illuminated the water several feet below surface where it struck. He thought it foolish that some passengers stood on the lower deck, dangerously close to the points of impact. The crew seemed not to even notice.

"How big is St. Louis?" Joshua yelled above a thunderbolt.

"Already close to a quarter of a million," Esther yelled in return.

"Seems impossible," shouted Joshua. "I didn't know there were that many people in all of Missouri."

"Do they treat all soldiers here in Keokuk or just Union men?" Grandpa asked.

"Men from North and South alike." Esther shouted back. Makes no difference their color neither….that's what I'm told, leastwise….. though I don't know if I b'lieve it. A surgeon who's a friend of our pilot likes to come on board to visit sometimes when we're stopping to refuel or let passengers off. He says President Lincoln is doin' all he can to impress on hospitals the need to treat all soldiers equally."

"That's the way it should be," said Homer with a courteous nod.

"Looks like we'll be here all night, folks….pilot doesn't like being away from shore in a storm." The chambermaid yelled to the entire dining area as she walked toward another table.

"Your mama's gonna hate spending more than she's budgeted for Burlington," Grandpa said.

"We're already planning for a night there, Grandpa. So why will it cost more if we get delayed?" Joshua wanted to know.

"Remember, trains don't run on Sunday. So we'll have a two-night stay," the old man said.

The delay wasn't all bad. The storm was over an hour later. Esther and the band provided music far into the night as guests dined on scrumptious catfish and elegant desserts.

They didn't get around to "Sweet Betsy from Pike" again until long after the younger boys were asleep—something for which

Lucy was grateful. She hoped never to hear that last verse again.

Except for a race with another steamboat, floating leisurely northward at mid-day on Saturday, nothing memorable happened for the rest of the trip except for a conversation that haunted Joshua long after he got back on dry land. It was between two men sharing a bottle of whiskey.

"I know everyone says the Union has this war won, but I think we've got a long ways to go yet. The South is going to fight to the finish. They are more interested in protecting their property than in protecting their own sons," one man suggested.

"You're right, Herbert," his companion agreed. "It'll be a sad shame if the Union is defeated. Above all, we must prove that Europe's wrong to believe that we can't have scores of states united into one country. We don't want another Europe. Just look how divided it is there, with all those tiny little countries."

"Very well said, Nicholas," Herbert agreed. "We're fighting to insure we have unity, and this country needs to expand. Unity is the most important purpose of the war, no matter what Lincoln says. He was smart to make the war about slavery, though. This insures the British leaders dare not support the Confederacy now. The populace in Britain would rise up in arms. I tell you, the Emancipation Proclamation is the final nail in the coffin for the South. With slavery detested by the common people of England, there's no way their leaders are going to join forces against the Union. Plus, King Cotton already fell from the throne. With the crop failures across the Atlantic these last couple of years, they desperately need wheat from the North more than cotton from the South.

"Well, Britain's not exactly been neutral in my opinion—between supplying arms to the South and allowing their ships to be built in British ports," declared Nicholas, getting louder

163

with every word.

Herbert hit the table hard and staggered to his feet as he brought the conversation to a close. "I agree, but I still believe unity is more than emancipation. If the slaves get free, that's fine," he yelled. "If not, we'll live with that, too. It's just not right the South should get by with spoiling what this nation was meant to be."

As the men walked off, arm in arm, Joshua looked at the stunned faces of Esther and the musicians, now working near the kitchen. Slowly, he scanned the expressions of other passengers, surprised to find most too absorbed in their own conversations to even notice what had just been said.

In Burlington, the family attended a church service that seemed void of political tension. Joshua listened intently, thinking how his father would love to hear this sermon on peace, so much like Rev. Miller used to give.

After church, back at the hotel, he pulled out his ammunition pouch and wrote a message, thinking all the while of his father.

Today we went to a church called "Old Zion." The Methodist minister told us: "Peace is normal. Fighting is not." It reminded me of you, Pa.

After worship, he told us that the two-story church has served many purposes since it's the largest building for many, many miles. It was once a school and has been a court house. In fact, a very important court house—the Iowa Supreme Court was meeting right there in the church when the court heard an important case back in 1839. It was called "the case of Ralph."

Ralph Montgomery was a slave in Missouri. His master trusted him to go work in the mines of Dubuque with the understanding Ralph would pay $500 for his freedom. He was to send the master money until the debt was paid. After some time, Ralph had still not come up with that sum. So the impatient master sent hunters to catch him and take him back to Missouri.

A kind Irishman, however, stopped them somehow. He got the judge to say they couldn't take the man further without going before the Court. Soon the court said he was free.

Ralph Montgomery was very grateful to the judge. One day the judge found him working quietly in his own garden. Ralph insisted he wanted to work for the judge for free one day of every year for the rest of his life because of what the judge had done for him. As far as anyone knows, he did just that. Ralph was one lucky Missourian.

Hours later, he remembered something else. "Peace doesn't sit and do nothing," the minister said. "Peace is always busy, actively working on problems that keep peace from happening." So he put this at the bottom as an afterthought. Later he would come to see it as the most significant of all the quotes he'd collected on the trip. It would serve to shape his decisions for the rest of his life.

That particular Sunday, he wasn't sure if reading was doing something active or not, but that's what he spent the rest of the day doing. He liked the kind, generous man who decided to buy Uncle Tom. Amazingly, it was because of his little girl asking that the slave be chosen just for her. She liked Uncle Tom instantly, and Uncle Tom liked her, too. While he longed for his own family, this little girl brought much joy to him for many years. She treated him like he was the grandfather she'd never met.

Closing the book, he began wondering about Ralph Montgomery? Was his family still enslaved back in Missouri? If so, Ralph wasn't so lucky, after all.

35

"The train in Missouri sounded 'ike it had a cold in its nose. Dis one sounds 'ike it's crying." The rest of the family, eager to board, simply smiled at Tom's cute remark as the train slowed and approached the station.

The man standing nearby, with a leather case in his hand seemed to think it a grand opportunity to start a conversation. "You're right, lad," he agreed. "I've traveled the rails all the way to the east coast and back. Every train has its own voice."

Tom was in awe. "How come?" he asked the expert.

"Much of the difference in sound is determined by the engineer. He sits up front and controls the whistle by a cord he pulls. It all depends on how long he holds it, or how hard or fast he pulls it. Like you, I think this one sounds quite mournful, perhaps like it's singing a sad song."

As soon as they boarded, the windows were all slammed shut except for Billy's. He declared the cold air wonderful.

According to the Burlington station master, he'd be stopping briefly twice before Mt. Pleasant, only thirty miles away. As it turned out, they hardly stopped at all. With nothing to load and no passengers to get off or on at the first stop, Joshua didn't even realize they'd passed the station.

He looked up from his book as soon as he heard the long, mournful whistle. "New London" the sign on the next station read. Yet less than a minute later, they were off again. Why so fast? What about the pile of wood beside the track? Suddenly the two men standing next to the wood pile ran toward the station. Craning his neck, Joshua watched in hopes of making sense out of things.

"Gunfire!" the man with the leather case gasped. Quickly, Joshua turned around in time to see two bullets fly past Billy's head. Fortunately, the seat in front, across from Billy, was empty. Yet the shots continued. Seconds after the first two, another bullet came through the side of the train, this time entering above Billy's window and landing near the car's entrance just as the conductor was about to step through from the front passenger car.

"Duck!" yelled the conductor as he lunged for the floor and stared at a spent bullet, inches from his face. His warning wasn't needed. By then, every passenger sat wedged between the seats.

Joshua glanced at his mother, working hard to stay calm while hovering over Jenny and Baby George, both crying. Looking back, he saw Grandpa protecting Tom in the same way.

The man with the leather case was the first to return to his seat, once they were out of shooting range. "What was that all about?" he asked. "I thought the bushwhackers stayed in Missouri."

"'Twasn't bushwhackers," the conductor explained as he dusted off his knees. "Maybe you didn't see the poor lady with two small children who boarded the car ahead of us. She was running from her husband and one of his friends. Smart lady.... had things well planned, made it to the station just in time for the train...not before her husband discovered his family gone, though....she told the station master that he hasn't been the same since he got back from a Confederate prison last year. Fortunately, the station master understood that she and her children were in danger and did some quick thinking, along with the engineer who got them safely on board. They're headed to her family in Ottumwa now."

The man with the leather case shook his head in disbelief. "Seems hard for some soldiers to return to peaceful living," he said solemnly.

His mother was one seat in front of him and across the aisle, so Joshua could easily see her face when it fell as the conductor spoke of prison. He wished she would tell him what she was thinking or more about what General Schofield had said. Being in the dark was worse than anything he might imagine.

Opening *Uncle Tom's Cabin*, he managed to read three paragraphs before he came to where Uncle Tom's tormentor was saying: "I've made up my mind to kill you." Replacing his marker, Joshua closed the book. He tried to focus on the ruby red foliage outside.

Meanwhile, Tom sat next to Grandpa, where they'd been since first boarding. "We can see so much more from here, Grandpa," he had argued when they chose the seat.

"Maybe so, Tom, maybe so.....just looks to me like a mighty fine place to sleep," quipped the old man.

Fifteen minutes later, Tom woke Grandpa when he jumped from his seat yelling, "Fox! It's Fox!" The rest of the family immediately joined his excitement as the child dashed up the aisle.

Of course, the man with the leather case was totally baffled. He might have easily thought the boy had spotted a red fox off in the woods, a common sight in those days. If so, he soon drew another conclusion.

"No, lad," he argued. "The Fox left Iowa years ago." Tom just stood there, looking forlorn as the man gently held onto his left arm, complicating things further. "Most of the Fox went to Kansas before I was born," the man explained. "No need to worry. Indians around here now are harmless. The one you saw won't bother you."

Lucy Carter didn't seem to hear, nor did she notice the problem at all. She was already at the door, about to step off the train. Billy heard. He looked back at Joshua in puzzlement, hoping his older brother would be able to later explain what on earth that man was talking about.

Grandpa, who'd been closely watching, was the only one laughing. Taking his time, he grabbed his knapsack, along with Tom's, and made his way forward. By then, Tom was out of patience. His scowl clearly showed it.

"Tom's not referring to Fox Indians, sir." Grandpa spoke politely as he stepped into the aisle. "He just saw his old hound dog ... by the name of Fox ... He's come to greet us all the way from Missouri." Grandpa squeezed past. His grandson stopped squirming and turned around as the confused man let go. The two men shook hands while Tom took off like lightning.

IMPORTANT: The strange man on the train might have thought he was an authority on the Fox Indians. They were far from finished with Iowa, however. Learn much more about these amazing people at:

http://www.meskwaki.org/History.html

36

"I'm sorry if you made a special trip to the station on Saturday. We were delayed by a storm," said Lucy to Olivia as soon as they were together in the wagon.

"Oh, it's good you were delayed," Olivia returned. "We didn't arrive in Salem until yesterday morning, so couldn't have come until today.... Turns out we got a place to live a mile from here, big enough for us all to share."

"Here in Mt. Pleasant?" Lucy was confused. "I thought we were settling in Salem."

"Another of our plans that got changed," Olivia said. "Salem's only ten miles south, though, and plenty close. We can visit often except in winter."

"What delayed *you*? " Lucy asked.

"Bushwhackers, after we got into Iowa," Olivia replied.

"Oh, no! I thought you'd be safe once you crossed the border. What did they want?"

"Mostly, they were interested to know if we were helping get slaves across the border....got a few dollars in the process....

169

thanks to you, not much, though. I sewed the money Mr. Johnson gave us into every garment we own."

The women laughed, then laughed again harder as Betsy whispered, "She even sewed it into her pantaloons."

"The good thing is they didn't hurt any of us," Olivia said, looking down at her daughter.

"People around Salem weren't a bit surprised to hear of our misfortune, though," she went on talking to her old neighbor again. "With their underground railroad, they've got plenty of stories to tell about troublemakers coming across the Missouri border. Don't worry. They've not experienced anything close to what Lawrence has. With most slaves either already sold or having run off, trouble has died down, too. Aunt Gladys tells us we should be safe in Mt. Pleasant."

"Who's Aunt Gladys?" asked Lucy.

Before Olivia could answer, they'd stopped in front of a big, two-story house with a dilapidated front porch. A good neighbor, driving a second wagon with the men and boys inside, hopped down to help Joshua with a steamer trunk. Soon everything the two families owned was sitting near the rear door of the house. Lucy, obviously puzzled and expecting answers, looked at her good friend.

"You see, "Olivia started explaining, "until today my Aunt Gladys has lived here in this old house where she raised her family," Until recently, they were able to help her more. Some have gotten sick. Others moved away. So she's been thinking she should rent her place out and move to a boarding house in town. That way she'll not have much housekeeping and can get good meals without having to cook. So when we got into Salem," Olivia went on, "someone suggested we come see my Aunt Gladys. She was thrilled to death, knowing that family would taking care of her place. We got her moved this morning and promised we'll soon have the old house fixed up real nice.

Life will be easier for her with her close to the shops in town, and she adores her new neighbors."

Meanwhile, Sam patted Homer on the back as the two stared at the dilapidated front porch. "It's near the schoolhouse and an easy walk to town, Homer. Plus, we got sixty acres of the blackest farmland on God's green earth."

"So, what do you think?" Lucy asked her father-in-law.

"Think? I'm not thinkin'.... just a'dreamin'," Grandpa said. "Also wondering if the man on the train will ever understand how old Fox managed to find us way up here in Mt. Pleasant, Iowa."

In November, the Mullins invited all their relatives for the first *official* observance of Thanksgiving. Just weeks earlier, President Lincoln had declared the fourth Thursday of every November a national holiday.

Lucy and Olivia bustled around, chattering incessantly about the fun this celebration would be. Their excitement spread quickly. Soon everyone was hard at work making invitations, decorating, cleaning, and cooking.

"You may notice something a bit odd with Quaker speech, especially with older folk," Olivia explained the night before the guests arrived. "They use 'thee' and 'thou' a lot. It's beginning to die out, but still the preferred way of speaking for many.... You'll get used to."

"Why don't you and Mr. Mullins talk like that?" asked Billy.

"We did as youngsters," replied Mrs. Mullins. "Growing up, we were also taught that every person's freedom of choice must be respected. So we exercised our freedom to speak like our good neighbors, once we got to Missouri. As you may have noticed, we didn't choose to do everything else like our neighbors or to think the same way, though. We basically kept our Quaker values."

"Can we try talking Quaker?" asked Billy.

Mrs. Mullins chuckled. "I wouldn't advise—might sound like you're making fun of them. It's just a sign of respect they show to one another."

Lucy declared everything perfect that first Thanksgiving morning. The huge, new porch took care of the overflow crowd. Nobody complained about the chilly weather. With hearts as warm as the bright sunshine, they were just glad it wasn't snowing.

With so many heartbreaking war stories, there was no want for conversation. People expressed hope, though, most of them confident the war would be over within a year.

The children spent little time listening to their elders. As soon as they finished their pumpkin pie, Billy started giving the visiting boys instructions for playing baseball. To his dismay, he soon discovered that the family's official diamond was taken. With the girls already into their second inning, the boys had to play their game near the outhouse.

37

By Christmas, everyone across the nation was chattering about President Lincoln's two-minute speech at Gettysburg, made just before Thanksgiving. Most newspapers printed all three paragraphs. School children worked hard to get the speech memorized.

"Out of all the words Lincoln spoke, the quote from the Declaration of Independence was most important," Grandpa said as he passed the mincemeat pie to his oldest grandson. "It's the Declaration that tells us what we must strive for."

"That's right, Grandpa," Joshua agreed. "As Pa always says, the problem is getting the Constitution to match the ideals of the Declaration."

"Yes, and I'm afraid we're going to be at it for a long, long time," added Aunt Gladys as she handed the pie on to Betsy.

"Hopefully, this is the last time our nation will be fighting a war about something in the Constitution, cause I don't think we can survive much more of this," Lucy Carter concluded.

Before New Year's Day, more sad news came—this time in a letter from Rev. Miller. Back in Jackson County for a visit, he and his wife had found the houses torched all along the Little Blue, same as throughout the evacuation zone. Though Order No. 11 was rescinded by late October—just six weeks after going into effect—there were only brick chimneys on the property of most returning residents. Referring to the famous Jayhawker who once held Wornalls captive, people sarcastically called them "Jennison's chimneys."

A late Christmas card from Aunt Charlotte was much more cheery.

Dear Lucy,

Hope everyone is well there. All of us are, including our new baby boy, born Dec. 16. We named him Cyrus. Thanks to the generosity of many people sending help from near and far, the store has been rebuilt. We are most grateful. Simpson is back at work and business is booming.

I am so worried about my dear brother. Please let me know if you get any news of him. Best wishes as you settle into a new life in Iowa. I hope we will all be together again someday.

Love,

Charlotte and family

*****

"Mr. Howe is the best school teacher in the state of Iowa," Aunt Gladys told Joshua in her persuasion speech before she took him to meet the head of Howe's Academy in early January. "I think you and I together can convince him you are ready for high school," she declared before adding her third selling point. "By the way, Mr. Howe took a group of students all the way to Lawrence, Kansas, to help with cleanup in the city's first raid, back in 1856. Knowing your pa went missing, trying to help those poor survivors this time … that should help convince him to give you more consideration, just in case he doesn't realize how smart you are."

Joshua was in awe when Mr. Howe agreed to accept him as a student. Knowing his family couldn't afford two dollars per week for tuition, he took a job delivering groceries. What impressed him as much as the scholastic opportunity was the way Mr. Howe believed in his students, giving each an opportunity to set the pace and select a course of study to pursue.

For a self-motivated boy like Joshua, it worked exceptionally well. Getting to know the hundreds of students, some riding long distances to attend, was as enriching as the studies. Like

Mr. Howe, Joshua loved to write about freedom. Journalism soon became his favorite subject.

One day he heard Mr. Howe talking about a young freedman yearning to study at the academy. Sadly, the boy couldn't even afford the reduced fee Mr. Howe offered him for attending. Joshua talked to his mother. He could manage fifty cents each month, if she could come up with the other fifty. Mr. Howe agreed to never let anyone know who'd helped him out. Joshua always said the eagerness he saw in the boy's eyes each morning was all the thanks he needed.

In early April, as he stepped out of the house on his way to school, mourning doves greeted him. It was a welcome sign of spring, but also served as a reminder of times past with his old friend Andrew Owsley. Somehow hope was born anew.

The world-famous Hutchinson Family Singers were soon due to arrive at the Union Block building in Mt. Pleasant. Joshua was overjoyed. Tom couldn't wait. He hoped they would take time to listen to him play the harmonica. Maybe they'd even let him play while they sang "Yankee Doodle," he suggested. Joshua just laughed. He only wished his father could hear the singers.

Since 1840, members of this family had sung reform songs across the nation—songs calling for temperance, abolition, and sometimes women's suffrage. At first, they shied away from abolition, fearing it would ruin their chances of becoming career musicians. Surprisingly, the outcome was the exact opposite. Although forced to cancel some of their concerts due to threats of rioting from pro-slavery groups, even in their home state of New Hampshire, the singers soon became famous, even helping President Lincoln win the 1860 election. Recently, several youth in the family had replaced the original singers, some dead and others no longer able to travel.

Their coming posed a sizeable dilemma for Sam and Olivia Mullins. Quakers in Salem cringed, hearing the news of "this evil" coming. Joshua didn't understand.

"Most Quakers see music, especially public performances, as worldly. They insist on being devoted only to 'things of the Spirit,'" Mr. Mullins explained. "That's where I beg to differ. Quakers talk about every person being able to 'follow the Light' as each sees fit. The Light for me is a world filled with wonderful music."

"So what are you going to do, Mr. Mullins?" asked Joshua.

"Why, I'm going to the concert," he replied. "What about you, Olivia?" he asked, turning to his wife. "Wilt thou be joining me?"

"Most certainly," she answered with a smile.

So, on May 2, Joshua thrilled at the lively tunes, but found the words of reform more intriguing. "There's a Good Time Coming," was his favorite song. It sounded very optimistic.

He jotted down one of his favorite lines: "Cannon balls may aid the truth, but thought's a weapon stronger." It brought back memories of Andrew watching the cannons at Lone Jack.

But the most memorable of all: "The pen shall supersede the sword." If ever he saw his father again, this would likely be the first thing he'd say to him after "Pa, I've decided to be a journalist like Mr. Howe."

While people in Washington and on the battlefields made difficult decisions in the hopes of bringing an end to the war, the Carters and the Mullins built a new life, thriving on the joys of safety and security.

They had plenty of time for fun, organizing baseball teams for both girls and boys while Aunt Gladys gathered a crowd for Saturday afternoon sing-a-longs in her old parlor.

They worked hard, too. The men and boys farmed and cared for their growing herd of cattle. Olivia and her daughters took care of household chores. Lucy's fingers were constantly sore from sewing from dawn to dusk. She could hardly keep up with orders while Sam stayed busy delivering her handiwork to every hollow for thirty miles around.

By spring, she saw an ad for a treadle sewing machine, made by Singer, a factory in New Jersey, now offering something no other American business ever had. They called it a "hire purchase agreement." Suddenly, someone like Lucy could obtain a machine with a small down payment, go into business, and pay out the debt with money generated from using the machine.

Lucy didn't know what Cyrus would think. Neither did she know what Mr. Wornall might say about her using the money he'd given her for something so risky. Well, neither one was around to ask, so she stepped out boldly and hoped for the best.

A few weeks later the shiny, black, metal machine arrived. Soon she was turning out fifteen to twenty garments each week. By the first anniversary of their arrival in Mt. Pleasant, she opened a shop next to the General Store on Main Street, naming it "Lucy's Lasting Stitches." She hired four freewomen and bought two more machines. Business was booming.

38

The whole house was abuzz. All through the fall of 1864, the excitement of preparing for their second Thanksgiving in Iowa far exceeded the enthusiasm of the previous year. The men delivered hand-written invitations all across the area in late September. Olivia Mullins had the boys washing windows while the girls scrubbed floors on their hands and knees. By the middle of October Lucy was calculating how many apple pies would be needed to feed seventy-five. She and Olivia would start baking several days ahead. Things could be stored out in the smokehouse, where they'd be well preserved, if not frozen.

There wasn't room, even in this big house, to fit all their new friends at one time. Guests from Salem were asked to come at noon, so they could get home before dark. People living closer would arrive mid-afternoon.

Added to the excitement, the new employees of Lucy's Lasting Stitches were coming and bringing their families. They lived at Lee Town, a short distance away, along with scores of other freedman families. Thanks to Mr. Lee, a builder and generous abolitionist, they enjoyed free land with many having free housing. "Free folks living on free land we are," the women at the shop often said for fun.

"'T'would be nice if ev'ry town in the nation had someone like Mr. Lee," declared Grandpa. "Those folks deserve assistance on the rocky road from slavery to independence."

Whenever Billy and Tom could get away from farm chores, they skedaddled over to Lee Town for a visit with Hosea and Truman Johnson. Hosea was Billy's best friend. Truman was Tom's. Billy taught Hosea and dozens of his neighbors to play baseball while the Johnson brothers taught Carters lots of new songs for Tom's harmonica.

Frequently, they told one another stories about their separate lives in Missouri and the challenging times they all experienced on their separate journeys to Iowa. Hosea especially liked to hear about Old Nelly dumping the wagon with Tom on top. Or about Joshua telling Frank Wornall he was almost fourteen and wouldn't be making Frank's eighth birthday party.

"How wonderful!" Lucy often exclaimed as she watched their budding friendships. "My children are growing up exactly like I dreamed of them doing for years, moving freely among all our neighbors."

Not everyone in Mt. Pleasant shared Lucy's vision. She realized this the afternoon she found Billy with red liquid streaming down his face from the raw beef liver Olivia insisted he put on his black eye. Like almost anyone could tell you, this was the best way to control the swelling.

"What did you do to get that?" Lucy asked her son, as if he was the instigator.

"Why do I always get blamed?" Billy complained as he always did, whether guilty of an accusation or not.

"Paul Bicker did it, Ma" Tom said, coming to the rescue from the next room. Billy listened gratefully to his little brother's eye witness account.

"Billy didn't do anything. He got socked because somebody spotted him from across the tracks last week while he played in Hosea's front yard," Tom explained. "Paul says to Billy, 'Don't you know Mr. Lee did us a favor by putting all them folks over there together?'... Then Simon Stockley puts his two cents in. He says 'Yeah, they got everything they need over there—even their own school. You better stay away from that place.'

"By then, with half the school gathered, everyone was chanting 'Frog Pond School! Frog Pond School! That's what they call it, Frog Pond School!' Next a punch sent Billy to the ground as three boys in big, deep voices bellowed. 'Croak. Croak. Croak.'"

Billy was smiling at his little brother now in spite of his pain. "That's when the teacher arrived and gave the croakers three afternoons of detention and blackboard cleaning," he added to finish off the story.

"Surely those boys will be ashamed if I tell them Hosea's story," Billy suggested that same evening to Joshua as the two talked things over at bedtime.

"It wouldn't matter, Billy," Joshua told him. "I don't think they have the courage to think about the pain of slavery or what it's like now for the Johnson family. Their cowardice is as bad as the slave holders."

Now, as Billy polished his mother's shiny, yellow fruit bowl in preparation for the big celebration, Joshua listened as his brother recalled how Hosea liked to tell his story.

"Pa was always taking Mr. Adam's grain to sell in Iowa," he'd say. "So the Confederates guarding the border knew him by name, usually just waving him on, knowing he'd soon be back with an empty wagon. They got fooled that day... didn't seem to notice Pa trembling so hard he could hardly hold the reins nor did they suspect the 'grain' under the scratchy burlap was alive ... cause we all held our breaths 'til we nearly busted. That's how Pa smuggled a-a-a-all of us and some of our neighbors to freedom. He didn't stop for ten miles, but when he did we like to never stopped whoopin'."

"You know, Joshua," Billy now said. "My school mates don't have any idea what they're missing by shunning the boys at Lee Town." He set the bowl in the center of the dining table and admired his efforts before moving to the next assignment.

Ma had asked him to make a "grateful list" to read to all the guests on Thanksgiving Day. He couldn't wait to see Hosea's face when he realized that his name was the first one on the list.

Although they centered their lives on things in Iowa, it was impossible to ignore present happenings in Missouri. Conflicts there were almost as intense as a year earlier.

The news sometimes came by letter, but more often through Mr. Howe. As an editor, he got word by wire before anyone else in town, often providing students sneak previews before the whole story was published.

Just Following Orders

"You won't believe what I learned today," Joshua told his grandfather as soon as he got home one afternoon. "General Price is back in Missouri, stirring up trouble again." He tossed his books on the desk near the front door, where he usually did his homework.

Grandpa groaned. "And I thought we'd seen the last of that man."

"Far from it," said Joshua. "He's got 12,000 men following him now, half of them guerrillas. They didn't encounter the reception they hoped for in St. Louis. So he's moving on, expecting to find plenty of sympathizers along the western border."

Price, a successful politician who had been governor of Missouri when Joshua was a small child, left the state at the start of the rebellion to become a Confederate general. Knowing it would probably cost Lincoln his chance for a second term, he was determined to take Missouri out of the Union. The entire nation held its breath, waiting for news.

Meanwhile, in late September, "Bloody Bill Anderson," one of Quantrill's best friends, led eighty men dressed in Union uniforms to Centralia, Missouri. They robbed a stagecoach there, destroyed train rails, and jumped a train filled with Union soldiers. Next, they set the depot afire. A company of Union troops saw smoke coming from the fire and went to investigate. When they found the bodies of twenty-three soldiers from the train, they took out after Anderson. In the end, guerrillas killed most of their pursuers, leaving over 140 bodies on the ground.

Price showed up in the headlines again, right before November's Presidential election—in a story about a huge battle at Westport, of all places. On October 23, he'd arrived there confident, despite having lost 3500 men from either desertion or disease. With the Union greatly outnumbered, things initially went well for the Confederacy. However, as more Union troops arrived, the tide turned. The Union prevailed.

Price's forces might have been totally annihilated, but most survivors managed to flee to Kansas.

"Mr. Howe now has more information," Joshua announced a few days later. "I'd love to talk to Mr. Wornall. It seems Price's men turned their Westport house into a hospital soon after the battle began. Yet once the Union started winning, they stormed in, shot any Confederate unable to walk out and turned the house into a Union hospital within minutes.

"I'm afraid such nonsense is gonna leave many folks with accounts to settle long after the rebellion's over," Grandpa declared.

Learn more about the history of Lee Town at

http://www.healthyhenrycounty.org/leetown.htm

39

A light snow fell the day before Thanksgiving. By afternoon, temperatures plummeted. Mr. Mullins went into town, anxious to get Aunt Gladys before the weather got worse. Closer to her aunt than any other family member, Olivia couldn't bear the thought of her missing the celebration.

"Tell her to bring plenty of clothes in case she needs to stay an extra night," Olivia instructed Sam. It was a good thing. They had three feet of snow by the next morning.

"Since when have things turned out like we planned?" she asked the children when they realized that Aunt Gladys was going to be their only guest on Thanksgiving Day.

"It's up to us to make the best of it all," Sam agreed. "We have everything we need for a long, lovely holiday."

"Certainly plenty of food ... could feed an army," Olivia declared as she put another log in the fireplace and poured herself a cup of coffee.

Joshua laughed. "Fortunately, an army stopping by is no longer one of our worries."

"And we certainly have no concerns about a water shortage," added Grandpa. "The way the snow's piling up, won't need to carry water from the well for weeks....got plenty right outside the door for cleaning, washing dishes, even Saturday night baths." With a sly grin he raised his voice on the last few words, looking toward the kitchen just in time to hear a groan from Billy, already standing with dishwater up to his elbows.

At Aunt Gladys' suggestion, Joshua strung a rope from the back door to the barn and tied a second from the barn to the outhouse. That way they could get out to take care of the animals and to empty the contents of chamber pots every day.

Grandpa thought it was a grand idea. "Taking care of chamber pots sounds like a good job for Joshua."

The boy made not a sound, just rolled his eyes and looked sideways at the old jokester.

"The important thing is for a second person to faithfully watch and wait inside the back door, ready to call for help in case the first one disappears," Aunt Gladys warned in all seriousness. "It's so easy to slip and fall if you drop the rope...easy to get disoriented out there, too. It can happen to the most experienced Iowan."

The children were forbidden to even put their heads out the door until further notice, leaving only their parents and Joshua for outside chores.

*****

"I wish never to see another bowl of squash soup or applesauce," Joshua grumbled two weeks later.

"It's all Olivia's fault," teased Grandpa. "If she'd sent *me* out before we had eight feet of snow stacked atop the cellar door, I wouldn't have followed orders as closely as you did, Sam Mullins." He jokingly glared at his long-time buddy. "Looks like you could have at least brought up a peck of potatoes along with all the squash and apples she ordered."

"You're right, Homer. It *is* Olivia's fault," Mullins said, extending his hands out, palms up, in resignation. He winked at his wife. She grinned back knowingly. "If Olivia'd given *me* the job of stringing up the Thanksgiving ham, I'm sure I would have hung it on the east side of the house instead of the north. Seems any fellow ought to know where the wind's gonna decide to suddenly put a drift so tall that the dogs can climb all the way to the roof for an overnight feast. "

Their undying humor made the monotonous fare bearable. They had flapjacks for breakfast one morning and gruel the next (with Tom insisting they call it "hasty pudding," of course). Noonday meals were just as monotonous as suppers. Squash soup, applesauce, and hardtack at noon. In the evening, a tall glass of buttermilk for each person with two pieces of cornbread crumbled into it. They fished the bread out with a spoon before drinking the remaining rich liquid that left thick mustaches atop every lip.

*****

"So what's Mr. Howe got you writing now, another paper on evil slaveholders?" Grandpa asked as he watched Joshua take from his desk a bottle of ink, two dip pens, and several sheets of clean paper.

"We never write about evil people, Grandpa," Joshua replied. "As I explained last week, Mr. Howe says the word "evil" describes bad things people sometimes do or say, not the people themselves. I think Mrs. Wornall's idea is important, too. Remember what she said about her father, how he'd had a long-standing habit of considering slavery acceptable? Well, it seems to me the habit of thinking in a twisted way often leads to evil behavior."

"You still didn't answer my question," the dear old man complained. "What is your assignment?"

"Sorry, Grandpa," said Joshua. "It's about reconstruction. Mr. Howe wants each of us to say what would best help the nation recover, once the Union finally wins the war."

"I'm glad to hear Mr. Howe is so confident of the outcome," Grandpa returned. "After all that's happened in Missouri lately, my doubts remain. I agree with those who say the South will be in complete ruins before the Confederacy surrenders, and that's yet to happen."

Seems to me helping the freedmen get jobs, like Ma is doing, should be a high priority," Joshua suggested. "It's more important than rebuilding structures, I think."

"But the freedmen can be put to work rebuilding structures, too," said Sam. "What so many are asking is whether freed slaves can really become responsible citizens, but I'm of the opinion we won't know until we give 'em a chance."

"The children won't have a chance to show us what they can do unless we give them good schools," Joshua said. "I don't see why they couldn't all go to white schools."

"It will be a lot of work for law-makers to find the exact words to re-write the Constitution," stated Aunt Gladys. "I think I'd start with that. Of course, no matter how they write it, people must be willing to abide by the law. Those with responsibility to enforce the laws must also find the courage to do their job."

Grandpa reached into a basket near the desk, pulling out a back copy of *The True Democrat*. "Did you see Mr. Howe's editorial about suffrage?" he asked.

"No, but I hope he's not thinking like those who say the Negro man should have the right to vote before we women get the privilege?" Aunt Gladys replied. "If so, then I need to have a talk with him. The new Constitution should grant suffrage to everyone at once."

"He also has an article about temperance," Homer continued, ignoring Aunt Gladys' point. "Now, that's something I'd like to see. Just think how much less violence there'd be if alcohol was illegal. Why, I doubt the guerrillas would be doing half the damage they're doing without the bottle as a companion."

"I also saw an editorial of his about abolishing the death penalty," Olivia said.

"Now, that's a radical idea," declared Aunt Gladys. "I never heard the like."

Joshua put his writing materials back in the desk. "Let's play dominoes," he suggested enthusiastically. He grabbed the wooden box from the second desk drawer and headed toward the dining room table. Surely there would be quieter days for writing before school resumed.

*****

One good thing about being snowbound was having more time to play. Dolls, jacks, school--those were the girls' favorites. Tom and his baby brother spent hours with wooden cars made from a growing collection of used spools their ma brought home.

Other old standbys included yo-yo's, dominoes, checkers, and jack straws. Most popular with the adults were Union playing cards, featuring army generals instead of kings and queens.

Every night after supper, Lucy lit a lamp for Joshua to read aloud from the past issues of the *Boston Commonwealth*. He tried to select articles and stories even Jenny could appreciate.

186

In early December, he started a story by Louisa May Alcott, published the year before. It came by installments, same way *Uncle Tom's Cabin* had first been published, one chapter per issue. Alcott's story was called *Hospital Sketches*. She based it on her own experience of nursing badly-wounded Union soldiers in Washington.

Jenny Carter was enthralled, despite the gory sights and sickening smells that had the young nurse in the story constantly spraying cologne all over the hospital. "That's what *I* want to do when I grow up," Jenny announced after the second chapter. "I'll go to Washington, sleep near the White House like Louisa, and take care of the poor soldiers."

"Imagine!" sighed Lucy, shaking her head in dismay. "A four-year-old.... already planning for a lifetime of war. Heaven help us!"

40

Two days after Joshua finished Alcott's story, Jenny started coughing. Nothing would stop it—not even the honey and sassafras tea. Desperately, Ma added onion juice and pinch of red pepper to no avail.

"Dr. Chilton's recipe ought to do the trick," Grandpa declared, handing a big brown bottle to Lucy. "Will cure anything that ails you, the peddler I bought this off of back in Missouri told me. I'd give her two big spoons full." Despite the little patient going into a deep sleep, her fits of coughing never ceased. She kept her worried mother up night and day.

Joshua often relieved his mama, sitting up half the night while he read *Uncle Tom's Cabin*. By skimming several chapters, he was determined to finish before Christmas. He skipped much of Uncle Tom's gruesome death and went on to the great ending.

All the while, Lucy kept wishing she could talk to Mrs. Johnson. That lady knew all sorts of cures. People around town considered her a miracle worker, some said better than any trained doctors this side of Keokuk.

Well, Jenny needed a miracle. She was only getting worse. So Sam ventured out and found Mrs. Johnson more than willing to brave the weather. She came with two bags, one with all her medicines, the other with clothes for her to stay several days if need be.

"Watch that skin carefully," she told Lucy. "This mustard plaster is powerful strong. T'will blister bad if you leave it too long, though." Jenny's chest was always a bright pink each time the plaster was removed, but her cough began to subside in a few hours. When she begged for hasty pudding, Olivia ran to the kitchen while Lucy danced for joy, gratefully sending the miracle worker home next morning with double the pay she would have gotten at the shop.

"If ya' got any ideas to stop this toothache, I'd be much obliged," said Grandpa, grateful to see the sun shining as he helped Mrs. Johnson into the wagon.

"Don't you know about Dr. Watkins?" she asked. "He's a freedman who came to Lee Town three years ago and now the best dentist in town—even uses chloroform for tooth pulling. White folks come for miles around to see him."

"You don't say. Well, where do I find him?"

"His office is in his house. It's a mighty fine place with big white columns, just a block north of the university. Hurry so you get that toothache taken care of in time to enjoy Christmas dinner," she advised.

On December 22, the children, except for poor Jenny, were

finally allowed to go outside—not for hours in the snow, as they'd hoped, but for thirty minutes in the barn with the animals. "That's where you belong, the way you've been acting." Lucy was in no mood for their grumbling, and she sure wasn't going to have another sick kid on her hands. "It's not my fault the thermometer hasn't moved above zero for four days," she told them.

The next morning Sam drove to Salem and distributed homemade Christmas cards, each with an invitation to come celebrate Christmas plus a late Thanksgiving as previously planned. Meanwhile, Grandpa took the Mt. Pleasant route. After delivering the invitations, he stopped in to see Dr. Watkins.

Lucy found a recipe for fudge. Despite the price of cocoa, she decided to splurge.

So did Grandpa. "Look what Dr. Watkins convinced me to buy," he managed to say when he walked in the door holding his swollen jaw.

"Merry Christmas to all," he added as he began pulling toothbrushes from each pocket. "Dr. Watkins says he doesn't know why he sells these things, beings they really hurt his business. I told him we'd all shared the same one on the steamboat, so I figured we could get by with just one here. He says it's much better if we each have our own, though."

"Wow, Grandpa! Thank you very much. What a Christmas!" the children kept saying while Joshua carved initials on the wooden handles to keep them straight.

They spent the next day stringing popcorn for the little pine tree Billy chopped down near their frozen pond. Joshua hung a six-foot banner in the dining room and asked for it to remain there after the holidays. On it, he drew a dove above his favorite line from *Hospital Sketches*.

"Peace descended, like oil, upon the ruffled waters of my

being."

Their delightful Christmas started bright and early when Mr. Howe, happy to finally be able to venture out of his house, stopped in unexpectedly with holiday greetings. He handed the latest issue of *The True Democrat* to Joshua. As Betsy helped him remove his winter gear, the journalist apologized for the paper being so late. He'd had it printed for two weeks. Oh, how he hated not being able to get this important front-page story to his readers until now!

The headline had Joshua puzzled. ""Sherman's March to the Sea? What's this all about?" he asked.

"The *end* of the story is yet to be written," Mr. Howe explained. "Sherman has 60,000 men marching through the South. Rather than fighting battles with the Confederate army, they're terrorizing any citizen who gets in their way, stealing and burning property to the ground as they go. He plans to continue until the South surrenders. I'd say it should be any day now."

"I wish I were so confident," Homer chimed in. "Being a southern boy myself, I know what a stubborn bunch of folks Sherman's up against." He chuckled. "Kinda like me."

"I don't know about stubborn, Grandpa," Joshua declared, "but you're sure persistent."

While sipping three cups of Olivia Mullin's sweet potato coffee, the teacher came up with an assignment that would keep Joshua busy for the next few days. He wanted a large map of the coastal states so the whole school could plot Sherman's progress.

"I have several more stops to make. I hope you enjoy the rest of the paper," he said as Joshua saw the guest to the door.

Back in the parlor, the boy opened to the second page of the paper, but quickly refolded it. Hastily, he tucked the entire issue under the tall stack of the *Boston Commonwealth*. He knew that what he just saw would devastate his grandfather. So today they'd enjoy Christmas. Tomorrow would be soon enough for the story of the Sand Creek Massacre.

Scurrying off to check out the luscious aromas coming from the kitchen, he tried to forget what had transpired in Colorado four weeks earlier.

*****

What happened at Sand Creek was every bit as awful as the Lawrence massacre. In fact, though it wiped out nearly as many lives, the victims were mostly women and children.

The genocide was provoked by men of two powerful professions. An editor in Denver called for "the extermination of the red devils." A Methodist minister by the name of John Chivington led the attacks. Chivington claimed that killing the Cheyenne was the only way to stop their resistance to "development."

The minister had a colorful past. In 1856, rebel congregants in Missouri threatened to kill him, same as Rev. Miller's congregants later did. Chivington's approach was quite different, however. He earned the title of "Fighting Parson" after entering the pulpit one Sunday morning carrying two pistols along with his Bible. He was quickly reassigned to Nebraska. From there, he went to fight for the Union in New Mexico before going to Colorado.

Joshua never did tell Homer what he read in the next edition of *The True Democrat*. His grandpa had hardly eaten for a week after hearing of the massacre. He certainly didn't need to know about the big parade in Denver, held to show appreciation for Chivington's actions. Yet the young student could hardly wait to get home the day he found out that an investigation

191

had revealed the minister's atrocious acts. In the end, he was kicked out of the army and never again allowed to return to the pulpit.

To **learn much more** about the Sand Creek Massacre visit:

http://www.pbs.org/weta/thewest/resources/archives/four/sandcrk.htm#editorial

41

On January 5, Lucy woke with a light heart. The sun was shining. She was ready to return to work, and Joshua wanted to spend the day visiting classmates to get help with the map.

At the shop, he built a fire while Ma pulled pieces for a fancy, satin evening dress from the cupboard and went right to work. Next, he drove to Lee Town to pick up her employees, brought them to the shop, and swung by the post office.

Though he stopped at the post office at least twice a week on his way home from school, seldom was there anything for them. When something did arrive, the whole family savored it like a rare treat. He never tore into a letter himself at the post office. Most were addressed to one of the adults, usually to his mother. The family would talk for days about the news, with the letter often read aloud several times as they savored every word.

"Something came in yesterday from the minister in Kansas City," the postmaster said, stepping behind the counter. "Envelope's so thin that it almost looks like he forgot to include the letter."

Joshua agreed. Very strange, since Rev. Miller loved to

write and normally sent interesting news clippings along, as well. Slipping the letter into his coat pocket, he thanked the postmaster and walked out.

His mind went back to the funniest letter he'd ever brought home. Arriving just before Thanksgiving of 1863, it was addressed only to Billy.

The boy had never received another piece of mail before. So, naturally, he had to share the funny story Frank wrote with everyone he saw. For extra measure, he told it to Aunt Gladys three times. Politely listening, she laughed with each telling as if it were the first.

Frank said that Hans hated life in Kansas City, so he went west with a friend before the Wornalls even got a chance to settle into the new house. Two weeks later, Aunt Molly, Jim, Pete, and Old Nelly just vanished on a Saturday night. Frank was the one who first made the discovery. His father, not believing it, went to check for himself.

Mr. Wornall couldn't understand it. Walking around in his Sunday suit, all dressed for church, he kept mumbling: "They didn't even leave a note."

Eliza had no problem cooking breakfast, of course. Fortunately, cooking was something she loved to do; but as they finished breakfast, she remembered the cows hadn't been milked.

So, without even thinking, John Wornall hurried to do the job in his Sunday suit. Guess he hadn't milked a cow in many years. He came back inside, his shoes covered with cow manure, his suit covered in milk, and hardly a drop in the bucket. So first thing Monday morning, Mr. Wornall hired a new servant, but he wasn't half as good as their old help.

*****

"What's Baby George doing out here by himself?" Lucy asked as Joshua stopped the wagon near the back door in the late afternoon. "The other children must have gotten careless and gone in the house without him."

Joshua jumped down, scooped up his baby brother, wrapped in three layers of clothing, and started toward the kitchen door as Lucy reached for her parcel. "No! No! No man!" screamed the toddler, pointing frantically toward the barn. Joshua laughed. His baby brother had never called him "man" before.

The boy's cries only became more frantic as Joshua reached out to open the kitchen door. He turned and looked toward the barn, where the child was persistently pointing, then gave in. As he followed the little guy's leading, it was obvious that he'd have to go behind the barn, not inside it, to satisfy the toddler.

Finally rounding the corner, Baby George squealed, clapping his little hands as his big brother stood gawking. "No man! No man!" he cried, pointing straight ahead. The "no man" was almost as tall as Grandpa.

Only then did Sam realize the child had been missing. He soon determined that the toddler had followed him to the house earlier when he went in search of two lumps of coal. Meanwhile the older children, intent with their snowman, hadn't been paying attention either.

"All's well that ends well," Joshua said, not wanting to think of how easily the ending could have been a disaster. Tucking his little brother under his arm like a big sack of potatoes, he joined the rest as they headed in for hot cocoa.

Inside, he hung his coat to dry and proudly spread the map on the table to show it off. After supper, Lucy pulled out the satin dress. She only had a few beads to attach across the front and hoped to start on it after putting the children to bed.

Just as the clock struck nine, she held up the finished garment to show Olivia.

"Tomorrow I'll have the money for this in my pocket," she said proudly.

"Pocket!" exclaimed Joshua. "Oh, I forgot!" He dashed to the coat-rack and promptly returned, handing the unopened letter to his mother.

"It's about time we got a letter from Kansas City," she said. "You read it, Joshua. I'm too tired."

Seconds later, Joshua let out a shout that had every child awake and running toward the parlor. "It's from Pa!!" he cried. "I'd know this hand-writing anywhere."

The note, first sent to Rev. Miller, had no date. Six lines were squeezed onto a tiny, old piece of paper with a torn corner. Yet it was the loveliest letter the family had ever received.

Dear George, Hope you can help me find my family. How I miss them! I've been here at St. Louis' Gratiot St. Prison 16 months. I survived smallpox. Since I have immunity, I get to care for others with the disease. Most of my hair has fallen out, and I'm quite thin. No mail goes in and out here, but I finally found a friend who knows how to get something out, anyway. No need for you to write. There's no way I'll get it. I hope to be home soon, wherever home is now. I'll be here waiting if someone can come as soon as the war is over. Surely it will be soon. Cyrus

Nobody slept for hours. They sang until midnight.

The next morning Joshua removed his father's note from the envelope to place it in the treasure box. To his surprise, he found another small note inside the envelope. "We have a fine, new baby girl, and the congregation has requested that we come back to Pleasant Hill as soon as the war is over to help make peace there." It was signed simply "George."

"He didn't have time to write." Lucy laughed. "Knowing Sadie, she's got him folding diapers and packing boxes at the same time."

*****

195

The household was aflutter for three, long months as they waited, hoping and praying for a rapid end to the war. Whenever it might come, Joshua and Mr. Mullins would be ready to go to St. Louis to bring Cyrus home. Lucy would need to stay and work. Grandpa, no longer up to traveling, would help Olivia manage things around the house.

Joshua soon had the details for himself worked out. As for school, students at Howe's Academy often dropped out for a term or two to save money for tuition. So dropping out to bring his father home was perfectly fine, Mr. Howe assured him.

"I must write Hector and let him know we're coming to Hannibal," Joshua said. "We can stop there on our way down."

As news trickled in, Joshua kept abreast of it all. The predictions of Mr. Howe and Grandpa were both right. In February, Sherman turned north to ransack South Carolina. From there, he tore through North Carolina and on to Virginia. Meanwhile, other Union troops were concentrating on Alabama, where the Confederacy held on long after April Fools' Day.

"It looks like a lost cause, but those southern boys will keep fighting like mountain lions long after this war is over, mark my word," Grandpa declared as he and Mr. Howe sat drinking coffee one Saturday afternoon.

*****

On April 5, two days after the Union took Richmond, Virginia, Lucy overheard Mr. Mullins and Joshua talking excitedly about their future trip as they played checkers in the dining room. Pulling up a chair, she sat and watched until the game was over before giving them the bad news.

"I saw Aunt Gladys yesterday. She was reading an article in the *Boston Chronicle* about prison problems. President Lincoln is declaring that each prison must plan to gradually release prisoners once the war is over. Otherwise, there will be havoc with so many hungry, sick men on the street at once. No matter what they do, many will probably die before they get home. The President hopes all the prisoners can eventually be sent home on trains or boats. That takes a lot of money, though...so it could be months before your father is discharged."

"Surely they'd release Pa if we're there to get him," Joshua said as tears clouded his eyes.

"We don't know, son. We just have to wait and see like we have on so many other things since your father's been missing," Lucy insisted. "You may be away for quite a while.

"Now, about the prisons," she continued. "General Schofield was brutal and angry when we saw him in Kansas City. I think he wanted to upset me as much as possible, and he succeeded. He bragged about the trouble your father would face, no matter what prison he might be in. He said that your pa was probably shot if Union men found him in violation of the draft. Until we got your pa's letter, I was afraid to even hope."

She reached for a morsel of cake from the plate in the center of the table. "Even if he made it to the prison gates alive, the general said he'd be more likely to get sick and die there than on the battlefield."

Joshua noticed her eyes. They were moist.

"So that's why you wouldn't talk about it all this time?" he asked.

She nodded, reaching in the pocket of her dress for a handkerchief. "That man called your father a coward and a traitor, and insisted that's what others would call him in prison and... " She stopped to gain her composure. "....long afterward if he should ever get out."

Joshua draped his arm across his mother's shoulders. "Ma," he said. "I've never told Mr. Howe why Pa is missing. Since he's such a strong abolitionist, do you suppose he'll think of Pa as a

197

coward and traitor?"

"No, Joshua," she said softly with a smile. "I know he won't. I've had some long talks with Mr. Howe about this. Like Mr. Wornall, he and your father won't agree on everything. But, also like Mr. Wornall, he's a kind, understanding person who respects people—especially teachers."

"We'll just have to remind Pa that *we* know who he is—a man with courage and guts," Joshua declared. "That's what's important."

*****

First thing, Monday morning of April 10, 1865, Howe Academy students were sent home as soon as they heard the news that had come from Washington to every telegraph station in the nation overnight.

"Peace has come! The war is o-o-over!" Joshua proclaimed at the top of his voice as he bolted down the steps of the academy along with all his classmates. He must have said those same words a hundred times as he ran through town, shouting jubilantly to everyone he saw.

Mrs. Johnson stood outside the door of Lucy's Lasting Stitches, grinning ear to ear. She waved as he ran past.

"Your mother gave us the day off, Joshua," she called out. "I think she's gone home to pack your pa's new clothes."

Without slowing his pace, he waved back, returning her smile. "Oh, no ma'am," he called as he rounded the next corner and turned toward Lee Town. "She has nothing to do but celebrate. Those clothes have been packed for weeks."

The church bells rang loud and long as if Christmas had just come to stay.

Epilogue

In spite of the pandemonium, Cyrus was released three days later, as soon as Joshua and Mr. Mullins arrived to ask for him. They didn't recognize the skin-and-bone man with the pock-marked face and no hair, but his voice and sweet spirit were still the same. Doctors at the prison hospital warned all prisoners to avoid big meals or rich food for several days because it would make them quite ill. By the time Cyrus got to Mt. Pleasant, though, he was ready for a feast. And that's exactly what he got every day for weeks on end.

How he missed his home along the Little Blue River! He longed for the familiar good times and seemed to almost forget the difficult ones. Yet his nostalgia soon faded.

It faded the day he learned of Missouri's *new* Loyalty Oath, this one even more incredible than the previous ones. For Cyrus, it meant he would have to sign an oath saying he had never been "disloyal" before he could return to teaching anywhere in the state. Even if willing to be dishonest, as so many others had been with oaths during the war, he ran the risk of again being imprisoned should his lie be discovered.

The family asked no questions, but often sat nearby as he rested, slowly came back to life, and began thinking of his own future. Meanwhile, he proudly watched his children play and his wife's joy and success.

"Let's see if we can round up some stones," he said as the leaves burst into brilliant gold and red. Soon they had a bench under a big walnut tree behind the barn. He spent hours reading additions Joshua made to the tin box, and answering his son's questions about documents he'd collected before his arrest.

Only rarely would he reveal anything about his prison experience until the day Mr. Howe asked him to be a guest lecturer at the academy.

It was a privilege Cyrus took seriously. He wanted to make sure students did not glorify the war or any war. He wanted them to understand the obligation America had to live for peace. Soon he began traveling to schools and churches, wherever he could find anyone to listen, spreading his message.

Most of all, he wanted children to appreciate their hard-earned freedom. Yet he couldn't help noticing how seldom those at Lee Town could fully enjoy the same freedoms as his own children. That concern became part of his message. Sadly, the message frequently met resistance.

Two years after returning home, Cyrus took Jenny with him on an important journey. They went to Muscatine, Iowa, to see Mr. Alexander Clark and his daughter Susan. Mr. Clark was about to go before the Iowa Supreme Court for what would become one of the most important cases in the state's history. He wanted his daughter to have opportunity to attend the white school near her home. Cyrus went with Mr. Clark all the way to the Iowa Supreme Court in 1868. The Court ruled that all Iowa schools integrate. *This was eighty-six years before Brown vs. Board of Education, the case that won the right for children of all races to be educated in the same classrooms.*

Mr. Clark wasn't the first African-American in Iowa to challenge school segregation. He was just the first to get his case all the way to the Iowa Supreme Court.

Many other parents had challenged it in local Iowa communities for years. Unlike in Mt. Pleasant, where schools integrated the year before the law changed, the vast majority of school boards refused to integrate. Even with the new law in place, few towns had people willing to enforce the law for several generations. Instead of welcoming the dark-skinned newcomers who had arrived as refugees, they chose to see the children as a threat to the "superior" white children whose parents had been newcomers a few years earlier. Davenport, for example, did not fully integrate until 1977.

Joshua completed college at Iowa Wesleyan, right there in Mt. Pleasant. As a student, he worked for Mr. Howe at *Iowa True Democrat*. Soon after graduation, he wrote for *The Saturday Evening Post*. Eventually, he became a journalism professor. Always, he kept in touch with his old friend Hector Collins.

Johnny became a professional baseball player. He later returned to Missouri, where he purchased farmland along the Little Blue River.

Tom wrote music for the Boston Philharmonic Orchestra.

Baby George finally got the family to drop "Baby" from his name, except when one of his brothers got in a teasing mood. When he finished at Mr. Howe's academy in 1879, George took off to Lawrence, where he lived with Aunt Charlotte and Uncle Simpson and was educated at the University of Kansas.

While still in college, George noticed something strange. In spite of that city's past passion for eradicating slavery, Lawrence did no better job of integrating than most other American cities. So he decided to become a school teacher, where he hoped to effectively work to integrate the schools as people already had in Mt. Pleasant, back in 1867.

Much of Jenny's inspiration came from her mother, of course. She was also greatly influenced by three others--her father, Mr. Clark, and a Mt. Pleasant resident by the name of Arabella Mansfield.

"Nothing in my life could top what happened in 1869," Jenny always said. "I was nine years old, but Pa tossed me in the air that morning like a feather. He told me I wasn't going to school. Instead, he was taking me to the Union Block building, not far from my mother's shop, to see Arabella sworn in as the first woman in the United States to receive a license to practice law!

From that day forward, I knew what I wanted to do."

As a student, Jenny often returned to the Union Block building to hear speeches by popular suffragettes who frequently gathered there. In less than twenty years, she had her own law license. Using that expertise, she worked behind the scenes with her favorite speaker, Susan B. Anthony. And she was *still* passionately fighting with other women for the right to vote in 1915, nine years after Anthony's death, when Joshua first told the story you have just read at a family reunion.

What's True and What's Not

On April 14, 1865—just four days after the Confederacy surrendered—Mt. Pleasant was in mourning along with the entire nation. President Lincoln had just been assassinated.

Look at the character list at the beginning of this book to see which ones really lived and which are a totally fictional creation of the author.

The 1863 Lawrence massacre, better known as Quantrill's Raid, did occur, as did Order No. 11. Both were horrific examples of how violence leads to more violence.

The story remains true to the facts of the Civil War, the bushwhackers named in the story, each of the generals, and the facts about Order No. 11.

John Wornall, an outstanding businessman, philanthropist, and politician, left a house that serves as a museum in Kansas City today. Though much of what is written about the Wornall family is speculation, the actual names and ages of the children were as written. Sadly, the two little girls were dead by the time their grandfather Rev. Thomas Johnson was murdered in January of 1865. Eliza soon joined them in death, six months after her father and just days after giving Frank a new baby brother. Both boys lived a full life.

In regard to the four ministers in the story, Rev. Johnson and Rev. George Miller were influential men of their day. The Shawnee Mission is an outstanding museum that sheds much light on its controversial founder. While the words attributed to these two are mostly pure fiction, all are based on research that makes their words plausible. Rev. William McGuffey's readers were used throughout the nation in public schools for much of the 19th century. Chivington was also a minister, just as the story says, when he led the horrific massacre at Sand Creek.

The shocking, initial apathy of area citizens was exactly as described.

Howe's Academy was probably the finest school in Iowa in the 19th century. Mr. Howe was the editor of *The True Democrat*. Following the 1856 raid, he did indeed take a group of students to Lawrence to help clean up. Mt. Pleasant is rightfully proud of how progressive the community was, with Lee Town and schools that integrated early and remained so. The historic Union Building still stands.

Influential writers of the day included Harriett Beecher Stowe, Charles Dickens, Samuel Clements (also known as Mark Twain), and Louisa May Alcott.

At http://justfollowingorders.takecourage.org, you can hear one of the many songs by the first popular singing group in the nation, the Hutchinson Family Singers. A library in Connecticut is named for Elihu Burritt. John Woolman remains known for his role in ending slavery among Quakers.

All of what's written about Captain LaBarge is true, including how the Sioux tried to kill the steamboat by putting out the fire in the engine. Also true, the horrific abuses against Native Americans and the failure of white men to keep so many promises.

Finally, believe it or not, the story of the little lamb who survived in the grill of the engine is true. You can find documentation of this at Patee House in St. Joseph, Missouri.

Many Thanks

Writing historical fiction requires a lot of networking, sometimes for years. It can even take decades unless a writer treats the project like a full-time job. That's what it fast became for me soon after I felt compelled to write this story.

"What you have here are two stories," Katie Armitage, a respected historian in Lawrence, Kansas, told me when she finished reading it.

"Of course," I replied, nodding in agreement. "Historical fiction is always two stories—the fictional one interwoven with the non-fiction."

"It's more than that," Katie explained. "You really have three here." She went on to explain that there were at least two stories that are important in history: the one about Order No. 11, the other about life in Iowa where the family found peace.

"There's a third one about protest," I later thought. It's people like Katie that have challenged me to think about the details of this project, encouraging me at every turn. She was the second historian to whom I turned shortly after discovering the true and tragic story of Order No. 11 that's interwoven with the story of the massacre, here in Lawrence, Kansas, where my husband and I came (from Iowa), expecting to merely retire in 2011—until I ran into the rest of the Lawrence story, Order No. 11, and knew I had to bring it to life for young people today.

The very first person I turned to after that discovery was Tom Rafiner, author of *Caught Between Three Fires*. Upon reading his chronicles of the many real-life people caught in the disaster, I was thrilled that he was willing to sit down with me for a long conversation. He patiently answered every one of my many questions that night and for weeks to follow, even before Joshua Carter's personality was fully formed in my imagination. The meeting itself was a gift, but the valuable maps he handed me were tangible treasures that would guide me for weeks as I plotted out various courses for my homeless characters to take.

Among countless other historians I consulted, several names stand out. There was Anita Farris at Shawnee Mission museum in Kansas City and Missouri historian Paul Kirkman, who saved me from going over an abyss or two as he discovered a couple of flaws in my research while reading one of the final manuscripts.

205

Dee Ann Miller

Frank Norris of the National Park Service in Santa Fe, New Mexico, taught me about the trail El Camino Real that brought so many foods and other goods to the southern tip of the Santa Fe Trail.

Museum personnel—both staff and volunteers—all over Missouri, Kansas, and Iowa deserve much applause for the way they responded to my questions, encouraging me, directing me to resources that linked me on to others in my quest to uncover every detail possible about the many themes in this text.

Topping that list is Emily Heid of Wornall House. Early on, Kate Gleason, acting as historian at Wornall House, took time for a long telephone visit after spending hours transcribing many pages of hand-written notes of Frank Wornall's memoirs that nobody had ever bothered to transcribe previously.

And how could I forget Pat Ryan White of Henry County for help in hammering out the many details of the fascinating history, as well as the physical characteristics, of that area.

At my most discouraging moments, I've gone back to May, 2013, when I sat next to Paul Bahnmaier at a luncheon and began telling him about the daunting challenge I'd given myself. Paul, the President of the Lecompton Historical Society is widely respected in Lecompton, Kansas, which claims to be the birthplace of the Civil War.

"Order No. 11? Why, that's the best-kept secret of the Civil War!" Paul exclaimed. While I'd already wondered myself if it might be, it was most validating to hear Paul say that.

Having studied the whole concept of secret-keeping and how it can create serious mental health problems in a family system, that statement really hooked me. I knew from that moment that I dare not abandon what I was doing, no matter how discouraged I might become.

And then there were the writers, school teachers, traveling companions, and students. Had it not been for Emily Heid, Dot Nary, Jean Grant, and Harlanne Roberts, I might never have found the voice for this book. They didn't mind telling me where I got things wrong initially. How I needed that!

Once the voice was established, I moved on to the hard task of finding the right words to succinctly convey the facts. That first chapter was re-written many times for days on end until just a few minutes before my daughter and grandsons arrived after a five-hour trip one evening. Within an hour of their arrival, I pulled 13-year-old Malachi aside and asked if he would mind reading what I'd worked all day to achieve. Malachi had no idea what he'd done for me as he looked up from the screen minutes later and provided multiple reasons why I'd managed to capture the suspense in those two pages in exactly the way I'd been hoping to. In those few seconds, he spoke with the authority of my target audience—something no historian could do.

So many thanks to Malachi and other young readers, some who read significant portions of the manuscript and offered feedback. These include Noah Cox, Cora Neher, and Madison Kuhle. Madison read the beginning chapters several times as it was still evolving, finished the entire manuscript and began "marketing" it to her friends long before it went to press.

Maggie Gilbert (aka. Steamboat Granny) steered me into understanding more about the adventures of steamboat travel. And my good friend Sondra Moseley, after decades as a band teacher, knew immediately what instruments I should place on the top deck of *Sweet Betsy*.

Other long-time teachers and reading specialists, Harlanne Roberts and Nancy Ketter, saw *Just Following Orders* as more than a novel. It had a lot of potential for classroom use, both insisted. Other educators agreed, like Annette Wertzberger, Rhonda Hassig, and Carolyn Hill-Demory, who each took time to read and add their own comments.

When Nancy suggested that I expand the project to add a second version for struggling readers and extensive lesson plans, I knew I needed help. How thrilled I was when she accepted the challenge to come alongside me as co-author! Her patience and faithfulness at every step has been astounding. She has endured more re-writes than I ever envisioned would be necessary, always sharing my commitment to accuracy, no matter how long it might take.

It was my life-long partner and sounding board for fifty years whose encouragement meant the most, though. I had no idea how much his degree in history had rubbed off on me. His ability to see old problems through new eyes came in very handy as so much of our table talk for many months has been about the lessons we've discovered together in this story.

Add to all of that the encouragement of many other family members and friends like Maria Vincent and Renae Cobb, who have all believed in me, added to the discussions, and kindly inquired about the progress of this fascinating project.

Thanks also to artist Susan Tower who generously offered her expertise in regard to the cover layout.

To each of these, I am deeply indebted.

About the authors

Dee Ann Miller has invested her life in cross-cultural mental health and community health nursing, much of it with troubled children and teens. She's also taught hundreds of children and adults to play the piano since 1995.

Seriously writing since she was twelve years old, Miller was first published in 1970, but her writing has always been for adults until now. Her last work of fiction is called "The Truth about Malarkey."

Her husband Ron is a retired American Baptist minister. His college major was history. Together they've spent many hours looking at the roles that religion has played in history and how it continues to shape our world today. Dee and Ron are the parents of two, the grandparents of five.

As a registered nurse holding a degree in behavioral science with community mental health emphasis, she has written on a variety of mental health and social issues, mostly with adult themes, since 1970.

Nancy Ketter spent more than a quarter of a century in fifth and sixth-grade classrooms. She holds a Kansas Certificate for Highly Qualified K-9 teachers, a master's degree in language arts, and has a very big heart for reluctant readers. She and her husband Phil have two sons and became grandparents for the first time as Nancy worked on the lesson plans along with this novel.

We're proud to provide teachers and youth leaders with prompt delivery of extensive chapter-by-chapter lesson plans FREE upon request. The plans offer multiple classroom activities. Also available is a four-session study guide for community youth groups. Submit your email request for either or both, with the code # 6114, using contact info at:

http://**justfollowingorders.takecourage.org**

Made in the USA
San Bernardino, CA
03 October 2015